I0534667

Seeking Skye

A Poppa Roy Mystery

Published by PMPEI Pty Ltd/R Addams
First Edition: January 2016
ISBN 978-0-9943452-3-3

Seeking Skye

A Poppa Roy Mystery

Prologue

I'm tired, but comfortably so

I've had a great life, managing construction projects in many unusual parts of the world. Now I'm retired, living in idyllic surroundings, and enjoying my life.

From time to time I've helped the local police investigate crimes, using my somewhat unconventional and unusual methods, but there haven't been many calls for my ability lately.

Then along comes Sue Weissman, a lady I probably don't remember as well as I should. Sue is a reporter for the Globe, a local paper.

Sue tries to interest me in investigating the apparent disappearance of a young local girl, Skye Burrows. There are no indication of any problems at home or at school and no evidence of foul play of any sort.

For some reason, I find the case a little intriguing but at the same time I question why I should bother getting involved. After all we have an entire police force asking questions of all and sundry and seemingly conducting a thorough investigation.

But certain aspects of this case don't quite ring true and I identify a few 'obvious unobvious' issues which leave me wondering.

This story covers my involvement in the search for Skye, the unorthodox methods I use and the various characters who help me in my quest.

Seeking Skye is a cute 'cozy' crime, (using the American vernacular), with some intrigue and just a little romance, and a dash of mysticism. It is suitable for all ages.

This is the first in the Poppa Roy Mystery series, but others are already on the way.

R Addams

Chapter One

Now where did I put that stupid pen?

The older I get I seem to lose things more easily, but it's getting harder and harder to find them.

Oh, here it is.

With pen in hand, I answer the telephone which has been ringing patiently.

"Roy Addams. Sorry I kept you waiting."

"Roy, Suzie here. Remember me?" The voice the other end sounds urgent.

The caller doesn't wait for an answer, and I hear, "Have you read about the young girl who has gone missing from Lismore? The one who's been featured in the local paper a few times recently."

It's Sue Weissman on the telephone. I remember her.

Well, I think I sort of remember her. If my memory is functioning well, I think she works for a local paper.

But I don't read the local one. Too much about issues which I don't think matter much in the overall scheme of things. Too many articles from people with vested interests and personal axes to grind.

"Err, hi Suzie." Fishing to ensure my sometimes unreliable memory is still functioning reasonably well, I add. "You work for the Globe don't you?"

"Yes Roy, you've got the right person. We met a few times a year or so ago, when you helped on the case of the stolen paintings. I interviewed you once before, about another case. But I wasn't involved in that one very much. Anyway enough of that," Now she sounds impatient.

"This is a new case Roy and one that has been in the news a lot lately. A sixteen year old girl is missing. She's been gone nearly two weeks now and the police don't seem to have many clues. None they are sharing anyway."

"Okay. If I understand you correctly Miss Weissman, you're telling me a young girl has disappeared from Lismore, and I should be interested for some reason.

Why, Miss Weissman? I mean, if the police are involved, why should I be interested? I'm just an old man. What's it got to do with me?"

"Roy, Mister Addams. To us at the paper, you're not just an old man. Far from it. Remember, we've seen you operate and we know how much you dedicate yourself to cases which interest you, and you seem to have a way of getting answers when other people can't. The girl's parents know you live in the area and they've told us they'd like you to be involved.

More correctly, the mother has. That's about where we are at the moment anyway.

What do you think?"

Funny question! I decide. I'm not altogether sure what she's talking about and I can't see why I should be interested.

I don't know what to think. As far as I'm concerned, I'm retired and I'm writing my memoirs. In reality, I'm supposed to be assembling my memories and records so I can write about them. I became involved in the case of the missing paintings as a favour to an old friend who owned the place they were stolen from.

"What about the police? How would they feel if someone from outside gets involved?"

"Well, I know you've worked with them before, but I haven't spoken to them about any involvement on this case at this stage Roy. But I'm sure I can convince them. There didn't seem much point mentioning it until I knew if you were interested."

That at least, made some sense to me.

"Can we please come and see you Poppa Roy?" Now Sue Weissman sounded less impatient, sweeter. "I hope you don't mind me calling you that. It's what I called you when we worked together last time.

I'd like to come and bring Skye's mother if I can. Skye Burrows is the girl who is missing."

I thought about it.

Do I really want to get involved in something new? Sometimes I feel I need something new to stimulate my brain into some sort of meaningful activity. Other times I wonder if I should bother. Why complicate my life with someone else's issues?

"Poppa Roy, Mister Addams. Are you there?" Sue is almost shouting. And sounding more frantic and impatient.

"Yes, sorry. Yes, of course I'm here.

Listen Miss Weissman, Suzie, I have no idea what this case is about, or why I should be interested. As long as you come to see me with that understanding, then yes, I guess we can meet, and you can call me whatever you like."

"Great!" Sue Weissman says. "What about ten o'clock tomorrow morning? Does that suit you?"

In all honesty my week is pretty well unscheduled so one day is as good, or as bad, as another. The time and days have become less significant than they were when I was younger.

"Fine! Ten tomorrow morning it is. And will I find much information about this girl if I check on the internet?"

"Yes, you should. Sue Weissman sounds a little peeved now. It's been in a few of the national papers, and ours of course, not that you probably read ours anyway. But you should find plenty. Skye Burrows, remember?"

"Yes, I have it written down in front of me. And I'll see you here at ten in the morning."

"Yes, Ten am."

"I have that written down too. I'll see you then."

We both hang up.

Turning to my computer, I decide I'll at least do some checking on this Skye Burrows girl.

I guess I owe them that much before I meet with them. But I'm still not sure why I should be interested.

Ah computers. With the world and all its information here right in front of me I'm enthralled, and so glad I became involved with computers and the internet as early as I did.

I detest the social media stuff though. People with too much time on their hands, as far as I'm concerned. Some with hundreds or thousands of so-called friends, whom they've probably never physically met, sharing meaningless tripe.

I once had an account with the largest site but I found most of the comments were basically just opinions, not necessarily with any factual basis. We all have opinions, always have and always will, but not all of us choose to put them out there for the world to see.

I read the news headlines on the internet occasionally, sometimes looking at the detail if the subject looks like it might interest me. And I try to answer the trivia questions in one of the national papers most days. It lets me know if my mind is still functioning reasonably well. But, apart from that, I use the internet more often for research and amusement. It's become my companion and a sort of replacement for my wife, to some extent anyway.

Marie died just over two years ago. Suddenly thank goodness. They said it was a massive heart attack. Strange though, because she never had any heart problems previously. I guess the doctors with their fancy machines, should know what they are talking about, although sometimes I wonder if they broad-brush a lot of things and give what they think might be the most easily understood and accepted explanation.

It was a pretty traumatic time and I'm glad Lisa, our daughter, was there to help.ᶦ She lives close by.

Marie didn't like computers. Didn't trust them either. She never really understood what they did and what huge amounts of information they could access. Even when I downloaded patterns and recipes for her. She would watch how I used a search engine to get the results I wanted, sorted the hay from the chaff, getting rid of sites which were just advertising, then printed the relevant pages. But she would never think of trying to use a computer herself. It remained something totally foreign to her.

There goes that telephone again.

"Roy Addams here."

"Dad, Poppa Roy." It's Lisa, my daughter, sounding excited.

"Dad, I was just talking with some girl friends about that young girl who's missing, the one from Lismore, and they asked me if you're going to be involved. Do you know the one I'm talking about?"

I look at the notes from my conversation with Sue Weissman. "Skye Burrows? Is that the girl you mean?"

"Wow! And I said you probably wouldn't even know about the case because you don't read the papers.

Does that mean you are involved dad? Is Poppa Roy going back to work again?"

"Not so fast Lisa, sorry. I've just had a call from that woman Sue Weissman, at the Globe and she's trying to get me involved. I've agreed to meet her and the girl's mother tomorrow. But that's my only involvement at this stage."

"That Weissman woman! I don't like her."

I'm not sure what Lisa is getting at so I wait. I don't think she'll be able to resist saying more. And I'm right.

"She's the one who wears short skirts all the time, and blouses that show off her tits. Most of my friends think she's a bit of a slut."

There, she's said what she thinks, and quite clearly.

I remember noticing Sue Weissman did seem to wear shortish skirts and revealing tops. She's one of those almost attractive women. I remember thinking that she had a pleasant enough face but she probably wasn't what you'd call beautiful or even really pretty. And that it was probably her legs and half-open blouses that got her attention, particularly from the police when we went to see them together. She always seemed to get their immediate attention, and cooperation.

13

"How long since you have seen her dad?" Lisa asks sharply. *I think it's almost accusingly, actually.*

I wonder if this is some sort of protection thing. Maybe Lisa is interested to check if I have been, or to make sure I wasn't, involved with the woman. I don't know Lisa's motives of course, but I answer her honestly anyway. I'm not the kind who plays games.

"When we wrapped up that painting thing, Lisa. When it was all over we had a photo session and the paper put the final story together. But I really dealt with other people most of the time. I think Sue was mainly involved on another story.

Why? What's the problem?"

"Oh dad. You may not be a young man but you're not in the grave either. And I know you get lonely with mum gone. So, well, I just wondered."

I guess that says it all, she's just being protective. Frustrating as it is at times, I know she means well.

"Yes. It does get lonely at times."

I couldn't disagree with that remark.

"I remember thinking that Sue Weissman did dress provocatively, but I'm not sure she's a slut. I honestly thought it might have just gone with the territory and she

14

dressed that way to open doors, sort of a sales tactic. I remember thinking that at the time at least, but I had forgotten about it until now.

Besides, I haven't seen her and I honestly haven't been interested in seeing her, if that's what you're getting at."

I think I stated my position clearly enough.

"Sorry dad. What you do is your business of course. I just worry about you sometimes, and I wouldn't like to see you get hurt.

When are you seeing them?"

I look at my notes again; to make sure I get it right.

"Ten o'clock tomorrow morning. They're coming here."

"Okay. Thanks dad. And will you call me afterwards and let me know what happens?"

"All of it?"

I decide to be a little cheeky with her.

Lisa laughs. "You old bugger! You know very well what I mean."

We speak about her kids. Michael, the oldest, is playing soccer the following Saturday and I promise to go and watch, then give him a ride home. It's important to be there, I know. Especially as Lisa's husband, Michael's father, works

15

away and can't make it back. He's a representative for a large American tractor company and is often required to work away from home.

We say our goodbyes and I promise to call Lisa after meeting Sue and Skye's mother the following day.

After hanging up the telephone I log into the internet and start my research.

Skye Burrows. A modern name, *Skye*, I decide. Sky without an 'e' used to be just the big blue thing up in the air and Skye with an 'e' was a place. An island, I think, in Scotland.

Surprisingly I find a few entries about people with the name Skye Burrows and I sort through various posts until I find some relating to a girl from Lismore who had just vanished, or so the reports say. *But no-one really just vanishes, do they?*

Logic says she must be somewhere.

I find some pictures and download them to my screen. She looks like a cute kid, probably a typical teenager. She's tall and thin with dark brown hair with a tinge of red, in a pony-tail in most pictures. Brown hair with some red colouring or naturally coppery, I'm not sure but it doesn't matter.

The reports say she headed to school one morning but didn't arrive, or, more correctly, a police spokesperson stated that no-one could remember seeing her at school that day, or since.

I assume from the articles, someone saw her leave home, but no-one saw her arrive at school. *My reasoning tells me therefore she must have gone missing somewhere between her home and the school.* I decide that, among other things, I need to know how far it is from her home to the school, and what streets are involved.

Also, do any of her friends live in those streets?

Being sixteen, Skye probably had a boyfriend. But there is no mention of one in any of the articles.

Did she?

Has he been interviewed?

I suddenly realize that I'm already getting involved.

If I'm seeing the mother and the lady reporter on the basis that I'm undecided, then I need to convince myself of the same thing.

Then why did I even bother beginning to research the case?

Getting up from the computer I pass a mirror.

Damn! I hope I don't have to get my hair cut.

I haven't had it cut for over a year now and it's just getting to a reasonable length. Well, what I call reasonable anyway. My hair is quite bushy and I tend to wear caps or hats, sometimes bandanas, when I go out, just to keep it tidy and to stop it blowing in my face.

People look at me quizzically, an almost seventy year old man with long curly hair.

An old hippy or someone who has just let himself go?

Neither really, I tell myself. Just a symbol of my non-conformism is my explanation, to myself at least. I can, so I do.

Anyway I decide, the length of my hair has absolutely nothing to do with my becoming involved in the case or, more to the point, how well I will perform if I do.

Other peoples' perception is their problem, not mine. I am happy with who I am and how I look. And besides, I wash it every day so it's certainly not a case of *letting myself go*.

Chapter Two

It's the day Sue Weissman and Skye's mother, are due to visit me, and I've checked my notes to make sure I've got it right.

I give the living room a quick spruce up, putting away some old newspapers and magazines and fluffing up the cushions the way my wife used to. I think it makes them too round and uncomfortable but women seem to like cushions looking puffy for some reason. I know they'll flatten themselves out again, so I don't usually bother.

A few minutes before ten, a car pulls up in front of the house. I'm sitting in a chair from where I can watch the street. I often sit there. It includes me in what's outside my window and my little world. But without me really getting involved.

I watch.

A woman gets out of the passenger's side. She looks about forty, smartly dressed in a long summery dress and cardigan. She looks at the house, closes the door of the car and waits for the driver to join her.

I see the driver is Sue Weissman. She's soon out of the car and walking around the front of it to, who I assume, must be Skye's mother.

I recognise Sue immediately. But despite Lisa's suggestion that she always dresses like a slut, today she's wearing a pair of what look like tailored slacks and a demure white blouse with a small jacket to match the slacks. A smart business suit I decide. The only thing possibly 'slutty' is her long mid-brown or dark blonde hair, which bounces as she moves, but to assume anything from her hair, would be a stretch.

The two ladies walk up my driveway and they're soon at the front door.

I open the door, still not really sure how I'm going to handle this.

"Hi Mister Addams, Roy," Sue Weissman is holding out a hand for me to shake. "Do you remember me?"

I take her hand and shake it politely.

"And this is Joanne Burrows, Skye's mother."

The other lady smiles and, looking a little cautious, she holds out her hand for me to take.

"Hi Mrs Burrows. And I'm sorry that Skye is missing. Come in ladies and please, call me Roy or Poppa Roy, whichever suits you."

I step back and let them enter the living room before me and select a seat.

Ladies first – old habits die hard!

Sue Weissman looks around the room. "No new woman in your life Poppa Roy?"

I am not sure if she has seen something out of place, perhaps some dust in an area I hadn't quite cleaned, or maybe she's just fishing.

I find it hard to read women sometimes. What they say is often not what they mean. At least that's the way it seems to me.

"No Sue. Probably not much chance there ever will be either.

Sorry ladies, but would you mind if I take notes?" I ask, picking up my note pad and pen. "I don't want to rely on my memory these days and this way I don't miss anything."

Joanne Burrows looks at Sue. I assume she's wondering if I'm still as good as people say I am. And it would be a fair enough question – *I'm not sure myself any more.*

"Go ahead Poppa Roy. Now, where shall we begin?" Sue is obviously taking the lead.

I write a few notes;

Sue wearing pants, not dressed as a slut.

Mother is Joanne. Looks pleasant.

21

Check dirt and dust in house.

"Mrs Burrows, perhaps you can start by explaining what you know. And I might interrupt and ask questions when I need to, if that's okay with you."

Joanne Burrows looks nervous, which I would expect and I can appreciate.

"Yes. Well yes I guess. But I've told the police all I know."

"Please remember, I'm not the police and I don't have access to any of their records. Assume I know absolutely nothing, which is pretty well the situation anyway."

"Fifteen days ago, Skye got herself ready for school and left the house the same time as usual, eight fifteen, to walk to school."

I hold up my hand. Joanne looks surprised but stops talking and nods.

I have just a few initial questions.

"Did you actually see her leave Mrs Burrows? I mean actually see her walk out of the house and along the street? And was she wearing a school uniform? Also, was she carrying anything apart from her normal school bag?"

Joanne Burrows looks a little strangely at me and I assume she has made all of this clear previously, probably a few times.

"Actually Mr Addams, Roy sorry, Skye came into the kitchen and gave me a kiss as she normally does. And I heard the front door open and close, but no, I didn't actually see her go. And when she came into the kitchen to say goodbye, she had her normal school bag, nothing extra. The school has a uniform jumper and the kids are supposed to wear grey pants or a skirt with the jumper. She was wearing a grey skirt or a full tunic. I couldn't tell which because the jumper was over the top."

I hold up my hand again and she nods again.

"And do any, or many, of her clothes seem to be missing?"

"None really. Which I thought was unusual if she planned to run away. If that's what you're getting at. Although, I can't find one swimsuit and there could be maybe a pair of jeans and some panties missing. She had so many pairs I can't be sure."

"Are you sure about the swimsuit?"

"Not really. She had a few pairs of bikinis and two or three one piece suits. A pair of bikinis seems to be missing

23

but she could have just thrown it away. There's no way I can really check.

Why? Could that be significant?"

I shook my head. "Probably not. Well, not that I can think of now, but it may be, so it's better to know.

So, Skye seems to have left the house at her normal time, although you didn't actually see her leave." I summarise and Joanne simply nods.

"Did anyone see her in the streets between your house and the school?"

Joanne shakes her head. "No, no-one. Well, no-one has come forward and claimed to have seen her."

"Doesn't that seem odd to you?"

I have no idea of the lay of the land or the distance involved but it seems odd to me that no-one might have seen her at what is possibly the busiest time of the morning, with people going to work and other kids heading to school. It just seems odd to me.

"Yes and no. Some people said they saw kids walking, presumably to school, and with their uniforms on. But when shown photographs of Skye, they said they couldn't identify her as one of the kids they saw. So the police have ruled it as inconclusive."

"And what about her father Mrs Burrows? Where was he, and did he see anything?"

Joanne looks at Sue Weissman. Sue nods and I assume I'm going to hear something that could be controversial, or at least, semi-confidential.

I'm right.

"Skye's father disappeared when she was about four years old. He said he was heading to South Australia to try his hand at opal mining.

Anyway, I haven't heard from him since he walked out so I really have no idea if he's alive, or where he is. I tried to trace him when I met Paul, Paul Burrows. I wanted a divorce.

All I managed to find out was that he was in a place called Andamooka for a few years, then nothing. Paul and I have been together since Skye was five. We're not married but I have changed my name legally, by deed poll, and Paul adopted Skye.

Paul has been her father ever since."

"Does Skye know? About her real father I mean."

"We haven't told her. So no, she doesn't know. Her relationship with Paul has been great and we didn't want to confuse the situation. Obviously we need to tell her sometime but we haven't decided when may be the best time. It probably will have to be before she gets married. We're not sure. We just thought it might spoil the relationship and we didn't want that."

"Okay, I understand the situation."

I didn't really, but I had more questions and wanted to proceed.

"What's the name of Skye's real father?"

Joanne looks at Sue again and Sue nods again. *Reassurance I suppose.*

"His name is, or was, Jan, Jan De Waal. He's Dutch but he migrated to Australia with his family when he was a kid. And yes, I've been in touch with his sister Marie, but she said she hadn't heard from him either, for over ten years. I also visited his parents when I was first trying to locate him but they claimed to know nothing then. And they're both dead now."

Joanne looks relieved, and I assume it's a part of her life she rarely talks about.

"So Paul, where was he?"

She knows what I mean.

"Paul left home just before eight that morning. I watched him drive out of the driveway, and I've been told he was at work in Ballina on time that morning, if that's what you are suggesting."

Joanne seems a bit tense and angry, assuming I'm suggesting that Paul may have been involved, I suppose.

"Joanne, please remember I know nothing and I'm definitely not suggesting anything. Where possible I ask questions to eliminate possibilities, and I'm sure the police do the same thing. It's one of the only ways we have to investigate, where there aren't any definite clues. We try to consider all possibilities, and hopefully, eliminate some as we go."

She still doesn't look happy and I soon find out why.

"The police have had Paul in the station twice, the last time for three hours. And they've interviewed everyone where he works. I've just about had enough of them insinuating that he might be involved."

"I understand. And I'm sorry if I'm going over ground that's been well trodden already. I just need to formulate my own picture of events. So please see my questions as that and no more. Because I know nothing, I need help to give myself a picture to look at."

"I understand." Joanne looks a little surly, defiant, and I understand after her explanation about the police investigating Paul.

"And I assume the police would have gone over this as well, and I'm sorry, but did Skye have her own telephone or computer?"

I know I'm probably going over the same ground again but I really don't have any choice.

"She has a mobile phone, which I've been trying to call but a message says it's switched off, or not in a serviced area. It's been the same message since, well, since she left."

Then a thought must have crossed her mind and she adds, "the police said they might be able to locate the telephone by its signal, but only if it's used. But it appears it isn't.

And yes, Skye has a note-book computer she seemed to take with her everywhere. It's not in the house, so we assume she has it."

"Have the police tried to trace if it has been used through its IP address or machine number, or even by checking whatever email or social network addresses she may have had?"

Joanne and Sue both look at me strangely. To me it's as if they didn't expect me to know anything about such things.

"Ladies," I try to pretend to be a little bit indignant. "I may be an old man but personal computers have been around for about thirty years now and I've had one since the first desk models were released. And I try to keep up to date.

I may not be an expert when it comes to some of the newer social network sites, but I can find my way around most things."

"Sorry Poppa Roy," Sue says. "Guess no book should be judged by its cover, should it?"

"The police said they were going to try to track it. If the note-book is used I mean," says Joanne, answering my original question. "But they haven't told me anything so far. I've asked three or four times, but I keep getting fobbed off. I'm beginning to think the local officers really have no idea, and it might be something they have only heard about."

"I could try to find out," Suzie offers quickly. "I have a good relationship with most of them and a few owe me some favours."

I can't help wondering why they would owe her favours but I don't dare ask. I decide to accept that we all

29

have our own methods and leave it at that. After all, I don't think either lady would understand if I tell them that one of my methods is talking with dead people.

Joanne's face doesn't show any reaction to Sue's remark and I guess perhaps her circle of friends don't share Lisa's opinion of Sue, or that Joanne wants answers, at whatever cost.

"I can also try. I've had some success in the past. Can you send me an email that you might have received from Skye recently?"

"Can you do that?" Joanne asks. "I had no idea."

"I can try,"

I really have no procedure I can think of, but I know the mysteries of computers would be more palatable, and easier for a person to accept, than my real methods.

"Do you know all of Skye's friends?"

"Yes, I think so. I've given a list to the police and I think they've interviewed all of them. She doesn't have a boyfriend at the moment but I've given the police details of the last two. I can send the same information to you as well if it helps, or get it to Miss Weissman."

"Please."

Now one of the big questions, one I have to ask.

30

"Joanne, do you know of any people Skye may have had problems with? Bullying and that sort of thing. And I realize kids can be cliquey and it can change from week to week"

"That's something else I've been trying to find out for the last two weeks. She certainly hadn't said anything to me, or to Paul. And the friends who I've spoken with say they're not aware of Skye having problems with anyone. Not this year anyway.

Apparently there was some sort of incident last year with a particular girl picking on Skye for some reason. Something to do with the boyfriend Skye had at the time, I was told. But her friends said the problem, whatever it was, seemed to go away and the girl in question left the school at the end of the year anyway."

"Can you find out that girl's name please? Including details of any of the other girl's friends who may have been involved. And let me know which boyfriend it was?"

Joanne nods. "The police don't have that information yet. Well, not from me anyway."

"It won't hurt if we're one step ahead in one small area. Although it may amount to nothing of course."

"What else do you need, Roy?" Sue asks, looking at her watch. "Sorry, but I have another appointment."

"A lot, but mainly what Skye was like. Did she play any sport? Did she have any girl-friends who were more special than others? What were her grades like at school? What do her teachers think? I need to know her.

And I guess the most important question Joanne, is what do you think happened? What could have happened, and in what order?"

All easy questions, although I appreciate the answers might be difficult.

I'm still writing my notes, and the questions, when Joanne answers.

"Skye used to play netball but not for the last year or more. I'm not sure exactly. She was particularly close to Rebecca Greene and Julie Tomlinson but they haven't been around home for a while so I'm not sure if that's still the case. She did very well at school and her reports indicate she was amongst the top in her class. I've spoken to a few of her teachers and they seem as mystified as everyone else. They certainly don't think Skye's school life was any reason for her to want to leave. Although one teacher, Carole Shaw, did suggest Skye seemed to be day-dreaming the last day or so. But that could mean anything.

Now, what do I think happened?

Even though it's getting harder as the days go by, I try to look at things logically. I think if someone took Skye there would have been some evidence, some signs of a scuffle, something. But there's absolutely nothing, nothing, to suggest that was the case.

That leaves the possibility that she wanted to go away and not be found, either with someone she trusted or on her own.

Honestly I think that's probably the case, that she is somewhere, hopefully alive and safe. But what I can't figure out is why. Why would she leave what was a happy home life?"

Joanne is crying by the time she finishes talking, and I can sympathise. I am not as convinced as Joanne seems to be that Skye is a run-away, although I can see her reasoning and I hope she's right. The fact that there are no signs of a struggle locally really means nothing. She may have left willingly enough then the situation changed.

One thing which bothers me is that, although Joanne is crying, and obviously distraught, her summing up of the situation seemed very clinical. Almost too clinical, as if she knows something more.

"One other question Joanne, if I may? Everyone needs money to survive. It's a basic necessity. Assuming you're right and she left home of her own accord, do you have any idea if Skye would've had any money she may have taken with her?"

"The police asked me that and honestly I can't be sure. She got money for her birthday, which was only a few weeks before she disappeared. And, as far as I know, she probably hadn't spent much of it. We went clothes shopping the day after her birthday but she said she couldn't find anything she liked. So she might have all or most of the money. I can't find it around the house anywhere."

"And how much are we talking about?"

"Between three and four hundred dollars I think. We gave her cash instead of presents. It was what she wanted."

"Did she say why she wanted cash instead of presents?"

"She said she hadn't bought any clothes for a while," Joanne replies, with tears in her eyes. "Which is true by the way. And that she intended to buy some clothes which could be mixed and matched so she would end up with a few new outfits. But as I said, the only time we went shopping together, she said she couldn't find anything she liked so she should still have the money, or most of it. And it would be in cash. She didn't have a credit card. "

"Okay Poppa Roy," says Sue, standing up and looking at her watch again. "Can you help Joanne or not?"

I look at my hastily scribbled notes. A lot of words with many question marks.

"Of course I can help, Miss Weissman. My question to myself at the moment is do I want to be involved? Is it a case that I want to be a part of?

And as it stands I'm still a little undecided."

"Do you, do you mean you can help find out where she is and what happened to her? I mean is it that simple? And what do you want?

We can't afford to pay you much at the moment, but if it's a question of money I'm sure we can raise whatever you want somehow."

"It's definitely not a question of money! I don't charge any fee, apart perhaps from travel costs if I have to fly somewhere, and accommodation expenses. Money is not the issue, it never is."

"Then what?" Sue asks.

"Ladies."

I don't really know myself, how to explain how I feel. I decide to just say it as it is.

"My methods include using spirit guides, which is something which you may not understand or agree with, I'm sorry. But when my guides believe they can help, I know I can help and I feel their power. So far all I have received from them are a lot of pin pricks, suggesting to me that they have more questions, and need answers."

Both of the ladies look at me as if I have more than one head, and I can understand that. And I guess I do have. The way I explained it anyway.

"So Roy," Sue speaks very slowly, "are you telling us the cases you've helped with before, and solved, have been as a result of contacting spirits, dead people?

Sorry, but that doesn't sound right to me.

Your answers and solutions have always seemed logically based, and you have presented solid evidence. I'm afraid I don't understand, and frankly, I'm not sure I believe you."

"Sue, Joanne, ladies, I don't really understand either, not always anyway. The simplest way to explain it is that I get messages and those messages give me directions, where to look and what to look for, that sort of thing. Yes I present my final solutions logically, but that part is easy because they are based on facts. Facts my guides help me uncover.

Why me? I honestly have no idea, believe me. It just started about ten years ago and they have never been wrong. Well, not so far anyway."

"This sounds too, well, it sounds too mysterious," Joanne says suddenly. "It sounds like mumbo jumbo and I don't think I believe you either Mr Addams!"

"I didn't expect you to Joanne, and I know that nothing I say to try to explain it better will change your mind, so I won't bother. But it's interesting. My late wife called it my mumbo jumbo too.

Going back to the basic question, yes, I can help, but I won't be able to tell you if I will or not until tomorrow morning. I need to do some thinking and to ask if they are interested in helping me, whoever they are.

I can only let you know after that. And, in the meantime, please don't say anything about this to anyone, not that they'll probably believe you anyway."

"You said they have questions Mr Addams." Joanne says. "Do you know what their questions are?"

"There is no commitment from them.

But I felt a tingle when Paul was mentioned. I think they want me to talk to Paul and to the officers handling the investigation. But I'm not sure what the actual questions are, not yet anyway. And from other sensations I felt, I believe I also need to talk to Skye's friends, and especially her ex-boyfriends. And, if possible, to the girl she was having problems with last year. Do you think any of those will be a problem to arrange?"

"No, not really. Although I'm not sure about the police, and I'll need to get the name of the girl and find out where she's gone."

"Leave the police to me," Sue says. "As I said before, some of them owe me."

"And can I have your telephone numbers please Sue, Joanne? I'll give you a call and let you know one way or another, let's say by around this time tomorrow. And I hope by then to have some idea of the order in which I need to see people."

Sue picks up her bag. She's ready to go. "Poppa Roy, Is this really how you operate? I mean is any of it you, or is it all some unknown spirit thing? Sorry but it seems so far-fetched."

I'm not about to detail my methods at this time but as I had let the cat out of the bag, to some extent anyway, I realise I have to say something.

"Sue, you know when you get a whiff of a story, perhaps a rumour, and you follow it through? You know what I mean? It may start off as a whisper, a rumour or an innuendo. It's a bit the same with me.

I obviously know the rudiments of conducting an investigation and I follow my instincts, a lot. But my friends guide me when I ask, or when they think I'm turning to them for answers, and they give me hints and suggestions. So it's both. Just me initially then me eventually, acting on their suggestions."

"Can I ask Roy?" Joanne seems intrigued. "Just how do you contact spirits? I mean is it like a séance, with a medium, that sort of thing?"

"Joanne, I can't give you any detailed explanations. And that's partly because it's not always the same way. Perhaps I'm better than I think and the inspirations comes from somewhere inside of me and I just call them my spirit guides. I don't know the answer, but there is definitely no séance, and no medium. It's just me."

The ladies leave and I watch through the window as they get into Sue's car and drive away.

I look at my notes, a scribble of points I got from Joanne's answers and questions. There are always questions. *Otherwise, if there were no questions, they wouldn't come and ask me to get involved would they?* If there weren't any questions the case would be solved.

Lisa, I must call Lisa, I tell myself. It's one of my first notes.

Lisa's house phone doesn't answer so I call her mobile. She answers it on the second ring.

"Hi dad. I am just having coffee with a few girlfriends in that little farm-house place we went to once. We were just chatting about the Burrows girl, and Sue Weissman. Are you going to take the case?"

She didn't waste any time in asking me. She always was a black and white person and very up-front. Like her mother, which I suppose is only to be expected.

"Ah Sue! Sorry to disappoint your ladies but today she was wearing trousers and a small jacket, over a blouse buttoned all the way up to her neck. She looked very demure."

I hear Lisa pass my comment to the others who are with her. I can't hear all the conversation but I make out the words '*mutton dressed as lamb.*' Obviously the other ladies had much the same opinion about Sue.

"And the case?" Lisa brings me back to her initial question.

"Honestly Lisa I haven't decided yet. Joanne Burrows seems nice enough, and I feel I may be able to help. I just need to sort out a few things in my head to decide if it wants me to follow the leads I have. I told them I'd let them know tomorrow."

"Yes, Joanne Burrows is very genuine, I think. Although I've heard a rumour that Joanne isn't married to that Paul guy. And that he's a bit of a strange one. He doesn't seem to mix with anyone else in town and I don't think he's got any friends." *Lisa's café set's gossip seems to be pretty accurate, about Joanne and Paul anyway.*

"Apart from the marriage thing, Lisa. This could be your mother talking, about me. She was forever criticising the fact that I didn't mix, and never joined local groups or clubs.

And as for their marriage thing, personally I think the fact that they've been together for more than ten years speaks for itself, and that's without a formal piece of paper or some words spoken by a man in a frock. Surely all of us should respect such a relationship."

Lisa is quiet for almost a minute, which is very unlike her.

"Okay dad. I guess you're right. They're together and they obviously suit and love each other, so what does the formality matter?

Anyway dad, my coffee's getting cold so I'll leave you now, but please, let me know your decision. And don't forget about the soccer game on Saturday."

"I won't forget. I've written myself a note."

As far as my mind at the time I have forgotten of course, but I have my notes and I know I put it in my diary, so I will be there.

Poor Lisa, I think.

Like a lot of people, she is very much a product of her social environment. The sort of person who listens to rumours and innuendos and accepts them as fact because the others in her social circle can't see things any differently. Issues are either black or white to Lisa, perhaps depending on the views of her friends, and there's not a lot of grey.

Still, I decide, *I love her.*

What I said about my wife is true. For years it seems like I rarely worked in the city we lived in, or even in the same country at times.

When we lived in Melbourne, my employer often wanted me in Perth, or running a project in Tasmania, anywhere other than in Melbourne. Then it was off overseas, to the Middle East, Eastern Europe and West Africa.

My spirit contacts started in Africa, I think.

My wife made a home wherever we lived and did her best to fit into the local social scene. I was never there long enough. At least that was my excuse. Perhaps I'm a bit of a recluse anyway.

Even in the last few years, work I've had as a consultant has been in Perth, Brisbane or Melbourne. Although it probably seemed like I was running away at times, it was just the nature of the industry I worked in, which was major industrial construction. To stay valuable in my clients' eyes, I felt I had to be available wherever and whenever they wanted me. Although, when I could, I also worked from home. But that also had its difficulties and still meant I was not out and about locally very much.

Chapter Three

I look at my scribbles and wonder again if I'm really interested in getting involved, regardless of what my guides might tell me.

If I say yes, I have no doubt Sue Weissman will feature me in her paper. That's what she does. Highlight the home-spun human interest angle of a local man and proven expert helping a local family in need.

I know I shouldn't have mentioned the contacting spirits bit. If that ever gets out my life could be hell, with all sorts of people wanting me to contact their dead relatives. Still, at the time anyway, it seemed appropriate to assure them they were dealing with more than just the old man sitting opposite them.

But I regretted saying anything, especially as I don't actually know if I'm really contacting spirits. I honestly don't know how it works and I haven't worked out a way of finding out how, short of finding a genuine medium. But I think the chances of me doing that are pretty slim.

I wonder just who or what I actually contact, if anything. Is it just me after all?

The telephone rings. Funny I can go for days without a single call, now this is the second or third call today.

"Hi Poppa Roy," I recognise the voice immediately. "This is Suzie again, from the Globe."

I am in awe. I was just thinking about her. Did I somehow contact her subconsciously? Are we on the same wave-length?

I don't know.

"Poppa Roy." She is whispering and I assume she's in a public office and doesn't want other people to hear.

"Did you mean what you said about contacting spirits? I mean, if you did, well, if you do, this could be a far bigger story than Skye Burrows. Don't get me wrong, finding Skye Burrows is important but this could be huge. "

I let this sink in.

Do or die time!

I know I need to get her mind away from the idea of spirits. The consequences of the Globe following up her visit with a story on me talking to the dead could be monumental.

I try to choose my words carefully.

"Suzie." I purposely use her more familiar name, "I'm not sure why I said that, perhaps so Joanne would feel that there isn't just an old has-been involved. Perhaps to off-set some of the blame, or credit if I am successful. I really don't know."

"So, are you saying you don't contact spirits? Is it just you?" Sue sounds disappointed.

"Without going into too much detail, my method, as I call it, involves writing out a lot of facts and questions, putting myself into a kind of meditative trance and waiting for answers. The answers come, or sometimes more questions come, but where from totally confuses me.

I honestly don't know if I'm being guided by something or someone external, or if it comes from somewhere inside of me. Some people call it spirit writing or automatic writing. For me, it began when I was in Africa and sharing ideas and experiences with a JuJu man, but I don't really know why it started. Maybe he gave me the ability. Sometimes it confuses me. Often it scares me because I don't know what it is, but it seems to work.

With the case of the missing paintings for example, something, or someone, told me to look for collaboration between the cleaning staff and security officers. I don't know what or who told me, or if it was just my logical mind. But when I began watching them and delving, doors seemed to open and I found there were leads which supported my line of enquiry, and clues just came. And you helped by asking more questions."

I hope I say enough to put her off, off of a separate story at least.

"So, what you are telling me now is, you really don't know where your inspirations come from?" Sue asks.

"That's it exactly. I really have no idea."

Oh what a pity!" Sue sounds genuinely disappointed and disillusioned. "I was going to suggest to the Globe that we should do an article or perhaps a series on mediums, stressing how they can work for the community and not be just fortune tellers. Without you, there wouldn't be much of a story. Everybody knows you."

"No Sue. There is no story. Not really."

"Okay, thanks Poppa Roy, and we will talk tomorrow?"

"Yes, definitely." I assure her. Then, looking at my notes, I remember something else.

"Sue, Suzie. Can I ask you something?"

"Sure, anything."

"Why did you assume there isn't a new woman in my life just by looking around the room? I mean, was something out of order? Did you notice something?"

Sue laughs and says quietly, "call it woman's intuition Roy. That's part of it. Besides, if there was a new woman in your life and you said you were entertaining two other ladies, I would have expected her to be there. But also I guess I was fishing. You're still an interesting man you know?"

With that she promptly hangs up.

I sit there for a few minutes, wondering if she's serious.

I don't know. And the thing is, I'm not sure if I want to know.

Chapter Four

It's late afternoon and the sun is beginning to set. I had a decent lunch, so I don't want to eat now. I've had enough for the day.

Going into my work-room, the room my wife used to call the study, I take out a note pad and a few pens. My scribbled notes and questions are alongside me, on the desk.

I turn on my computer and find the icon for my mantra, on the computer's desk-top. I tend to keep files on the desk-top if I use them regularly. It seems easier than filing them away then having to remember where they were filed. The mantra helps me focus. At least I think it does. I don't seem to be able to work without it.

On a blank sheet of paper I write *Skye Burrows*. I miss a line then on the next one I write *Is Skye Burrows alive?*

Then. *Where is Skye Burrows? Is she alone? Has she been hurt? Why did she leave?* On and on I write questions, on every second line a question.

I look at the paper and see I have written out fifteen questions but then I realize I haven't explained who Skye Burrows is, which Skye Burrows?

As I saw on the internet earlier, there are others with the same name.

Starting at the top of a new sheet of paper, I write a brief introduction then rewrite the questions but with more detail, enough to give me, or anyone else, enough information to know the Skye Burrows I'm referring to is the one described in the introduction.

I throw the original sheet of questions into the cardboard box I use as my rubbish bin and start a new page. I write more questions; *were either of her parents involved in her going missing? Did she have a good relationship with her mother? Did she have a good relationship with her step-father? Has she seen her real father? Is either man involved in her disappearance?* Then, repeating myself I know; I write, *Is Skye Burrows alive? Is she okay?*

Where is Skye Burrows?

I now have two sheets of paper with a question on every second line, my starting point.

I look at the clock, seven thirty. Time to see what answers I get.

I get up and switch off the main lights. The only light now is from the next room. Clicking the computer mouse, I bring the black screen to life again and begin to concentrate on my mantra.

It's action time.

I hold my pen. It hovers over the two sheets of paper, which are side by side, taped to my desk. I'm ready for some inspiration.

The telephone rings.

Damn! I forgot to unplug it from the wall, as I usually do.

"Hello, Roy Addams speaking."

"Mr Addams. This is Sergeant Barry Fletcher from the local police Missing Persons squad. How are you this evening?"

It sounds like a man's voice, but it's slightly muffled, not clear.

But maybe it's my ears. After all, it is getting late for me.

I don't know a Sergeant Fletcher, and have no idea why he might be calling me. My instincts tell me it may be something to do with Skye Burrows, but I don't know. I decide to be polite and to let him talk.

"I'm fine. And how are you Sergeant Fletcher? Or should I call you Barry?"

"Barry is fine, and I am well," the muffled voice says, then nothing.

He doesn't say anything else, and I wait patiently, although I'm actually getting a bit impatient. I want to go on with my exercise on Skye Burrows.

After what seems like a long time, but was probably only a minute, he says, "Mr Addams, we understand you may be getting involved in the case of a missing girl, Skye Burrow. Is that correct?"

There! He said the magic words. This is about Skye Burrows after all.

"Actually, I haven't decided yet. Is there some sort of problem if I were to be involved?"

"Let's just say we would prefer it if you don't." The voice says.

"Sorry, but who are *we*?" I wonder just who I might be up against, and why.

"As I said before, I'm with the Missing Persons squad."

"Listen Sergeant, I don't know much about the case and I honestly have no idea yet if I'm going to get involved."

And I hang up.

It's annoying. On the one hand I've got a woman who seems nervous but very sincere, and Sue Weissman, both begging me to get involved. And now someone is trying to warn me off becoming involved.

I decide to call Sue.

I find her business card and call her mobile number.

"Hi Poppa Roy. To what do I owe this pleasure? I honestly don't think you've ever called me on my mobile before."

"Sue, do you know a sergeant named Barry Fletcher? He just called and suggested I shouldn't get involved in this case."

"Poppa Roy, I know all the guys in the local police station, some better than others I admit. But I don't know anyone named Barry Fletcher. It's not a name I've even heard of, so I don't think he exists. Not unless they've brought someone in recently from Sydney or from somewhere else. But I'm fairly sure I would have heard if that was the case.

Can I call you back in a few minutes? I'm going to call Ken Wood, the boss of the police up here. He'll tell me if anything's going on. And, if he asks, can I tell him you're in?"

"Not yet Sue, sorry. I still haven't had a chance to well, to sort myself out. But can you call him this time of night?"

"Don't worry about me Poppa Roy. Most men are quite happy for me to call them at night. I'll call you back."

With that she hangs up, leaving me a little more confused.

Is she a slut, as Lisa says or does she just use her feminine wiles occasionally, sort of on the basis that the end justifies the means?

I honestly don't know and again, I'm not certain that I want to know. Maybe her methods are like mine, something that shouldn't be explained or discussed.

I look at the mantra on my computer screen, a little wistfully. I should be getting on to the case, and it frustrates me that I can't.

My telephone phone rings again.

"Poppa Roy," Sue Weissman sounds excited. "Poppa Roy, I think we have a problem. There is no Sergeant Barry Fletcher on this case, and Ken Wood has never heard of him. I explained you might be getting involved and he seemed keen but, because someone is obviously warning you off, he

54

wonders if it's a good idea. For you to be involved I think he means. He's thinking of your safety.

Phew! This is becoming more involved."

"It certainly sounds like it. I wonder who the person who called me really is, and why he wants me off the case? Do you have any idea, Sue? I mean who knows that you and Joanne came to see me anyway?

"Poppa Roy, my editor knows of course, but I haven't mentioned it to anyone else at the paper, just in case you didn't agree. And I don't know who Joanne might have told.

But I'm going to find out." Sue sounds more determined now.

"And Ken Wood is going to check if there is a Sergeant Barry Fletcher in the force somewhere. Maybe another division is involved without him knowing, for example, but he thinks that's an outside possibility at best."

I think it through quickly.

She's right, it is becoming more involved.

"Please don't mention anything to Joanne.

For one thing, if someone she knows is desperate enough to do this and he knows we're on to him, he might do something more desperate, to me, to her or even to you. I honestly think, whatever happens, we don't mention it and keep any involvement on my side very low key. I have to give it some more thought, but at the moment I think we shouldn't publicize it at all.

I know that the paper will want a story but maybe you sit on it until there is an outcome, then you will have a much bigger story wrapping up the entire case."

"Are you telling me you're going to take the case?"

"Sue, I did say '*whatever happens*,' and I meant if I take on the case, or if I don't. I honestly haven't had enough time alone in my old head to decide anything."

Sue and I hang up. She may use questionable methods but she's like a terrier with a bone, I decide. She doesn't let go, doesn't give up. Which is probably a desirable trait in her profession.

I'm about to unplug the telephone from its socket when it rings again.

"Dad, dad, what are you going to do?" It's Lisa and she sounds excited.

"What do you mean Lisa?"

"I mean are you thinking about taking on the case of course!"

"I still haven't decided, Lisa.

Why, is there a problem if I do?"

56

"Dad, I just had a call from a police officer named Barry Fletcher." Now she sounds frantic. "He said they don't want you involved and that he spoke to you but you hung up on him."

Now how much do I share with her? I wonder.

I decide to say it as it is.

"Lisa, I just told him the truth. That I don't know what I'm going to do, then finished the call. There was really no more to add. But I've checked with Ken Wood, the local police chief and there is no Barry Fletcher in his station, or on the case, as far as he is aware anyway. But he's checking further."

Lisa is quiet, letting my answer sink in I guess.

"But dad!" She says. "That's worse. Some guy who says he's a police officer is threatening you and somehow he's got my number as well. This is terrible."

"Lisa, there was no threat. Not to me anyway. And you haven't said there was any to you. Now the police know about him I honestly don't think we have anything to worry about."

"Dad, I just hope you're right. Good night now, and please be careful."

I assure her I'm always careful.

I'm probably not of course, but I can't tell her that.

I look at my computer screen. The mantra image has disappeared again. I look the blank screen wistfully. I know I should get on with my work but decide I had better check all the doors and windows first, before I unplug the telephone.

We only have two outer doors and I make sure they are both dead-locked, something I very rarely bother with. Then I check the windows. Some have locks fitted, and I make sure these are locked. In most of the windows however, there's just a piece of wood in the frame, to stop the movable pane from being slid open.

I check all the pieces of wood are in place. One's missing for some reason and somewhere in my mind I remember using the piece of wood for something, but I can't remember exactly what for now.

It's only a small window and I look around for something else, anything, to jam in the window frame. I settle on a pair of long-handled tongs, barbecue tongs I think. They are basically the right length and, with them in place, the furthest an intruder might slide the window open is about three centimetres. *Not enough to do any damage* I decide.

I am being careful, I tell myself.

Back in front of my computer, I unplug the telephone from the wall socket. It hasn't rung since Lisa's call.

With that deadened, I hit the RETURN key on my key-board and the screen comes to life. There's my mantra. It's a fairly simple one which I've found to suit me and my purpose best. I've never been sure if it's Hindu or Muslim but it works, so its origin has never really seemed important.

I take up my pen and poise it over the two sheets of questions. *Time to get to work.*

I study the mantra, first the shapes, counting how many triangles there are, and how many diamond shapes, then circles and squares.

Then I study the different colours, how many red objects in total then how many red of each shape, then the blue.

Fairly soon I don't know what I am looking at, or why. I'm not there anymore.

I start the process just after eight pm, maybe eight-thirty, and when my head clears I see from the clock on the screen that it's almost ten-thirty. I've been somewhere else for about two hours.

Chapter Five

I switch on the main light and look at the sheets of paper.

There's writing in different places, but not against all the questions, and it looks as though the answers have been written by several different people.

Different people?

Written in different hands is probably a more correct way of putting it. There's no-one else here so obviously *I wrote them all.*

Some answers are directly under the questions, which is of course easier for me to follow. There are other words written haphazardly across the page, which makes them hard to align to specific questions, and two words are upside down.

I start from the top of the first page.

Is Skye Burrows alive? This is my simple question, after the explanation of which Skye Burrows I'm inquiring about.

The response is clear and concise **YES**. Nothing confusing or inconclusive about that response, I decide.

Where is Skye Burrow? This didn't get the same unequivocal response. What is on the paper is a series of five

question marks, each a little larger than the previous one.
?????

Sometimes I had considered the question mark as indicating that the spirits – or whatever they are – need more information. But then there's usually a question somewhere on the sheet of paper. I look at all the spirit writing, turn the paper sideways and upside down but I can't find any question which might be appropriate to my original one. *Not very helpful*, I think.

Is she alone? This was probably a silly question from the outset. I know what I meant – *was she actually with someone? Did she leave of her own accord?* – That sort of thing. The response underneath my question is **NO**.

Again, clear and concise but because my question is ambiguous, the answer is probably equally so.

Has she been hurt? I decide, after reading the question again, that this one too is ambiguous. The response is a clear **YES**, but I realize the answer could relate to Skye being hurt at any time during her sixteen years, and may not have any bearing on the current situation. Also it may mean being hurt emotionally as opposed to physically. I write myself a note, to be less general and ambiguous with my questions in future.

Why did she leave? This question gets a series of question marks as well, but again I can't find any further words which might refer to it.

I run down the page and look at the other responses. *Were either of her parents involved in her going missing?* The response to this one is interesting. There are two question marks and a fairly definite '*no*' - **??NO.**

Some of the scribbled comments on the pages are neither responses nor further questions, in fact they don't seem to refer to the specifics case at all.

BE CAREFUL, DON'T TRUSTANYONE and **DON'T BELIEVE THEM.**

These all leave me a bit confused. I have no idea what or who the comments refer to specifically, who are '*them*' and what constitutes '*anyone*?'

There is a response to *Has she seen her real father?* The response is **YES**, but again, my question was not specific as to the time period I'm inquiring about.

I had knowingly repeated the question *is Skye Burrows alive?* And the response is the same as before, a clear and concise **YES.**

Is she okay? This is another of my later questions, on the second sheet of paper. The response is long and confusing.

GIRL IS SAFE. GIRL IS NOT IN DANGER. GIRL IS NOT OKAY. GIRL IS ALRIGHT.

From these responses I gather that although Skye is not in danger and she's safe, there is some problem. *I wonder what that could be.*

I look at the reply to my second question about Skye's whereabouts. *Where is Skye Burrows?* This time the response is one question mark and a word – **?NORTH.**

I make notes from the various responses, Skye is alive, she may be somewhere north; which could mean almost anywhere in the world, she has met her real father sometime or other, she is safe and not in danger but she is not alright.

The only other things I conclude are that neither of her parents were probably involved in her going missing, that I may be in some sort of danger and that I shouldn't trust or believe anyone.

Past my normal bedtime I notice, looking at the clock again. I decide to sleep on the responses and ask more specific questions in another session in the morning.

Then an odd thing happens.

I punch in CTRL, ALT, DEL, intending to turn my computer off, but the keys have no effect, and my mantra stays on the screen. I try again, and again nothing happens.

It seems the computer wants me to stay on line and doesn't want to switch off.

I'm tired so I hit the power on/off button and pull the cable from the rear of the computer. I watch for a few minutes. The screen goes black, then there is a tiny white spot in the centre of the screen, until finally it goes to sleep, which is where I want to go.

Chapter Six

I'm in bed but I don't fall asleep. Not immediately anyway.

Skye Burrows is alive, but I haven't been told where she is, other than somewhere north. I wonder where she could be. A lot of places are north of Lismore. It could be somewhere close like Bangalow, Nimbin or Byron Bay, or somewhere further away like Surfers Paradise or Brisbane. I decide north is not a very good description and that it needs further questions.

I've also been told she's safe, she's not in danger but that she's not alright. I wonder if that means she has been hurt so she is not okay but that she is not in any immediate danger. Or perhaps it means something totally different, perhaps not okay emotionally.

And, what am I going to tell Joanne Burrows and Sue Weissman I wonder? Actually I wonder a lot about Sue Weissman. *Just who is she, and what is she really like?*

I decide I need to get to sleep, be up early and try to meditate again, with some less ambiguous questions. And hopefully get some more specific responses.

Finally I drift off to sleep.

o0o

I wake about seven, get up and put the kettle on. Coffee first thing in the morning is one thing I know I can't do without.

I've had my coffee, showered and I'm dressed by eight, and now I'm facing my computer again. I plug it in and switch it on.

While I wait for it to boot itself up, I take a clean sheet of paper and start writing.

I begin again from scratch, first writing out a similar preamble to that I used previously, to try to avoid any ambiguity. Next, my questions.

Is Skye Burrows alive?

Where is she?

How far from Lismore is she?

Did she leave Lismore of her own free will?

Did someone help her leave?

Was she happy at home?

Was she happy at school?

Is she happy where she is now?

Does she want to go home?

Is she free to go home or wherever she wants to go?

Has she been physically hurt since she left home?

Can I find her?

Who do I need to talk to?

Who can help me find her?

I figure these are enough questions and that, if all questions are answered reasonably unambiguously, I should know if it's worth me going further.

I look at the telephone and realize I've left it unplugged all night. I decide that if there was anything important, someone would've been pounding on my door by now. But they haven't.

Bringing my usual mantra up on the screen, I wonder if I should try to make the room darker somehow. I've never tried to contact the spirits, or whatever they are, in the daytime. I look around a few times and come to the conclusion that it doesn't matter.

Mindful of the time and the fact that Joanne and Sue are likely to be at my door within two hours, I try to concentrate exclusively on my mantra again.

After going through my colours and shapes routine, I begin to try to assess if there are more triangles than diamonds, and are there more circles than squares?

I am awake. I think I have been meditating, or somewhere else in my brain anyway. It's nine forty-five, almost time for my visitors. Looking at the single sheet of paper I see there's writing on it.

Is Skye Burrows alive?

YES

Where is she?

NORTH

How far from Lismore is she?

CLOSE

Did she leave Lismore of her own free will?

~~**YES**~~**, NO**

Did someone help her leave?

YES

Was she happy at home?

YES, ~~**NO**~~**, YES**

Was she happy at school?

NO

Is she happy where she is now?

YES, ~~**NO**~~**, YES**

Does she want to go home?

~~**NO**~~**, YES ??**

Is she free to go home or wherever she wants to go?

??????

Has she been physically hurt since she left home?

68

???NO!!!!

Can I find her?

??YES

Who do I need to talk to?

DON'T TRUST ANYONE!!!!!!

Who can help me find her?

YOU

I read through the responses again and, again I look for other comments on the paper.

There are a lot of words, some of which seem to be sentences or phrases but none which appear to make sense, except one **BARRY FLETCHER IS NOT!!**

Are they telling me that he is not a police officer, or that he is not to be trusted? Or perhaps both? Or maybe that he's not Barry Fletcher at all. Often the responses I get confuse me and this is one of those times.

I read the responses again. She is *close* to Lismore, and *north*. The response regarding if she left Lismore of her own free will was changed from **NO** to **YES**. Does that mean she didn't initially, then did, or perhaps that she never actually left Lismore? *Is that why she's close?*

The answers appear to suggest that Skye is alive and that I can find her, somehow.

69

Also that I shouldn't trust anyone, which is a bit of a mystery to me in itself; there is no definition or limitation on *anyone*. I wonder if that also means I shouldn't trust myself and my own judgement.

I look at the clock again, *almost ten*.

I can't remember if Joanne and Suzie are going to visit me again at ten, or if I'm supposed to call them. I have their numbers and I decide I'll call them if they're not here by ten fifteen.

Then I remember the telephone's not plugged into the wall socket so I plug it in and check the call register.

It says that I've missed two calls, one last night and one this morning, but both callers are shown as '*Unknown Number*' and there are no messages.

Not much point wondering who it might be, I decide. *If it's important, they will call back. If not, it doesn't matter.*

What am I going to say to Joanne and Sue Weissman?

I weigh up what I know again. If Skye is alive and if my spirits tell me I can find her, I think, *why not?*

Then I remember this Barry Fletcher guy. And he has called Lisa. *Should this worry me*, I wonder?

Thinking that someone is trying to scare me off, and suggesting I shouldn't get involved stirs me up a little. I've always resented anyone telling me what to do or what not to do. I think I'll get involved on principle. Just to irk this Barry Fletcher, whoever he is.

Yes, my mind is made up! I'm in.

Ten past ten now, and they haven't come or called me. *Perhaps I did promise to call them after all.*

If it is to be, it is up to me! I remember hearing or reading that somewhere and I think now, how well it describes my present situation and my intention to be involved. I take it to mean, quite simply, that it's up to me to make something happen, if I want it to happen. It's pretty basic logic.

I don't hear or see a car pull up, but my door bell rings.

Sue Weissman is at my door. She's alone.

Following my daughter's assessment of Sue I take notice of what she's wearing, but I don't think I ever really did when we cooperated on that previous case. I can't really remember, so obviously it couldn't have seemed important or significant at the time. But I remember too, that it wasn't long after Marie's death.

This morning Sue's wearing a shortish skirt, not indecent but hemmed above her knees, and a plain pink button through blouse or shirt. And it is buttoned up. I assess her as being dressed reasonably demurely.

"Well Poppa Roy, what have you decided?"

Sue comes straight to the point after we shake hands and say hello. My memory tells me she has always been direct and to the point.

I invite her to sit and ask if she would like a cup of tea or coffee.

I need to get my thoughts together before I answer her question.

"I'd love a cup of coffee. Would you like me to make it?"

"No, my pleasure." I wander into the kitchen to fill the kettle, switch it on and rinse out the coffee plunger.

Sue follows me.

"Have you made up your mind Poppa Roy? You did say you would let Joanne know this morning, but I can put her off if we need to. It wouldn't be a problem."

I busy myself putting a small jug of milk, spoons and the sugar container on to a tray, then add two mugs.

"If you can take these into the lounge room, Sue. I'll bring the coffee in a few minutes and we can talk. And no, there's no need to put Joanne off, but thank you."

Looking a little confused, Sue takes the tray into the lounge, and stays there.

Okay! I tell myself. *Just tell it as it is.*

"Shall I pour?" Sue asks when I put the plunger on to the tray with the other things.

"Please."

In reality, errors of parallax sometimes occur and I can rarely pour things without some spillage, so I'm glad she offers. Besides, I'm a little intrigued at seeing Sue in a domestic role, no matter how minor. It is so unlike the brusque, business-like persona I would normally associate with her.

I've managed to pick up my cup of coffee without spilling a drop.

"Sue, I think I know that Skye Burrows is alive."

I'm careful not to say I believe, I think or I know. This way I'm not telling Sue that I know Skye is alive, or that I just think she's alive. It's somewhere in between the two.

"Right. Go on." I have her attention.

"I consider I can help, in fact I'm sure I can help. And I've decided I want to help. But it must be on my terms or I'll walk away."

"Okay," Sue says patiently. "I really don't know what you're getting at as far as your terms, but I'm listening."

"Sue, because that guy Fletcher, or whoever he is, called me, and he's also called my daughter, I don't want the fact that I've agreed to be involved to be made public."

Probably the worst thing to tell a reporter who survives on telling news and stories, but it's how I feel.

"In fact it would be great if there's a story stating that I'm working on some other case, and simply can't be involved. That'd be the best, if I can think up another case."

I watch Sue and let my condition sink in.

"Poppa Roy." *She's looking cagey. I think she has some sort of angle.* "It's going to be difficult to hide the fact you're involved if you start asking people questions, as you said you need to, but I think we'll probably be able to find a way to work around it.

But if I can convince the paper not to print anything, and to publish a statement that you can't be involved for some reason, can I have your guarantee that you'll give me a detailed, step by step explanation of your investigation, your methods and your conclusions?

Also your agreement that you won't discuss the case with representatives from any other paper, or radio and television reporters? We would expect an exclusive."

My turn to smile. Sue's reply is exactly what I wanted.

"That won't be a problem Sue. But I'm not sure you'll get much out of an explanation of my methods. But maybe I'm wrong. As I said yesterday, my wife used to call it my mumbo jumbo, bless her soul. She never tried to understand. But then, she thought the same about computers."

"You can trust me," Sue says. *And immediately I recall the warning. 'Don't trust anyone.' Where does that leave me? I wonder. I have to trust someone, sometimes, don't I?*

"Can we put an agreed basis of our understanding in writing?" *I'm not really sure if she will agree, but I don't know how else to phrase it.*

"So you don't trust me?" Sue sounds a little indignant but she has a grin on her face. "If that's the way you need it Roy, we can type something up, but as long as you understand I probably won't have the final say and that it must be subject to my editor agreeing as well."

"If we prepare a document and sign it indicating our agreement, can you get your boss to countersign it?"

I thought that might upset her but it doesn't seem to. She seems to think the final revelation would be something monumental that she could use. But I find out she's really protecting herself.

"Of course." She says. "That way the paper won't be able to go behind my back either. The agreement will make it clear it will be my exclusive story. Can we type something up now or should we call Joanne Burrows first and make sure she's on the same page?"

I hadn't really thought the Joanne aspect through at all.

Then I realize we have to tell Joanne something, but if we do, there is always a risk that she might say something to someone.

Sue's right. Joanne has to agree as well.

I think about the situation. I initially consider perhaps we shouldn't tell Joanne, but reason with myself that probably wouldn't be fair.

"Do you think you could get Joanne to come over here? Maybe we can get her agreement at the same time."

I realize I am probably being hopeful, but I can't think of any other way.

"I can try." Suzie says. Give me a minute."

She takes out her telephone and dials a number.

"Hello, Joanne? Listen hon, I'm here with Poppa Roy. He is still deliberating whether or not to take on the case, but he needs to talk with both of us, together, before he can decide. He's explained the issues to me and I agree with him. Can you get over here, or can we come there. Or, if necessary, I can collect you and bring you back here.

You can? Fifteen minutes? Okay, great, see you then. She's on her way."

"As I said last night Suzie, I don't think we should mention the Barry Fletcher thing to Joanne. Firstly it might scare her but more importantly, she may tip the person off, perhaps inadvertently, or if she knows who he is. Or even thinks she knows."

"What about your daughter? Lisa isn't it? How is she about all of this?"

"Lisa knows that Joanne came with you yesterday, to speak with me. But she doesn't know my decision, and I won't tell her. I'll think of some excuse.

77

And because this Barry Fletcher guy called her as well, she has some idea he may be a problem. And I told her that Ken Wood said there's no Barry Fletcher involved on their side so she knows it is something other than a police issue.

I think it will be easiest for me to say I'm not going to get involved because of Fletcher, or until we can sort out who Fletcher is. It'll sound more logical to her that way."

"Lisa. She doesn't like me, does she?" Sue asks.

"The only excuse she could have for not liking you is that she doesn't know you."

I don't believe Lisa has any real justification for not liking Sue.

"Roy, I've seen the way Lisa and her coffee-set cronies look at me. They think I'm something else. And, in all honesty Roy, it doesn't bother me. I do my job and I think I do it well. If that doesn't suit them, that's their problem not mine, unless they have shares in the Globe of course." She laughs at this.

"Shall we try to get some words on paper before Joanne comes?"

I want to change the subject, away from Lisa and her impression of Sue.

78

We go into my work room. My spirit pages are still on the desk but I cover them with the blank writing pad before Suzie has a chance to study them.

I sit at the computer. When I hit the ENTER key, my mantra occupies the screen.

"That's pretty. What is it?" Sue looks at it closely. It is obvious she likes it.

"Mmm, let's just call it a study aid. It helps me concentrate."

The ESC key gets rid of the mantra. I select WORD from the bottom tool bar and a blank Word page opens.

"You're probably the better typist Suzie. Why don't you type out what you think we've agreed to then we'll review it and make changes if necessary."

She agrees and we change places. Suzie sits at the computer and her fingers fly over the keys. After just a few minutes she prints out a full A4 page of words, something which would have taken me perhaps half an hour to type then another half an hour to edit and correct.

I read through the words. She has captured basically what we said and the only aspect I ask her to change is the reference to Lisa. Sue included Lisa as a signatory, on the assumption that Lisa will know that I'm involved and that she would have to agree to keep quiet about it.

I assure her, and I thought I already had, that I won't tell Lisa and will use the Barry Fletcher guy as the reason.

Sue smiles sweetly. "I thought you said something like that. I was just covering all the bases."

"What about Paul, Joanne's partner? Do we need to include him?" Not having met him, I'm not sure where he might sit in all of this.

"Let's wait and see what Joanne says," Sue suggests.

I am about to say I agree when we hear a car door slam.

Joanne is here.

Chapter Seven

Sue and I meet Joanne at the door.

Joanne looks nervous, which I think at first is totally understandable, but then the *'don't trust anyone'* aspect kicks in and I can't help wondering if she's really what she seems to be, a grieving mother.

I'm not sure what it is, but, for the first time, something about her doesn't ring true.

We say our hellos as people do, then sit in the lounge, as Sue and I had done before. The coffee things are still on the table and I ask Joanne if she would like tea or coffee. She says no.

"Mrs Burrows, Joanne. Firstly, I am reasonably sure that Skye is alive and secondly, that she's alright."

Joanne Burrows bursts into tears when I finish talking, and I immediately wonder if my suspicions about her being something other than just a grieving mother are reasonable. She appears relieved, and distraught at the same time.

"Where is she?" Joanne Burrows manages to say through the tears.

"First things first, Mrs Burrows, sorry. I believe I can find Skye, but we asked you to come over here for a specific reason. I'm agreeing to become involved in the case but subject to one very strict condition, and only if all parties, which includes you, agree to my condition."

"Of course. Anything. Just find her please, and bring her home."

"The condition is that no-one can know that I'm involved. There can be nothing in the Globe, or any other media, which suggests I'm connected with the case. Which means that you can't tell anyone that I've said yes, not even your partner, Paul. You can tell him I'm being an obstinate old man, or that you simply don't believe I can help in any way. Tell him anything. Anything, but the truth of course.

And, for my part, if Miss Weissman and her editor guarantee not to release anything about me being involved, they'll get an exclusive story, detailing precisely how I go about solving the case, everything in detail. They, or more specifically Miss Weissman, will have a world exclusive and I guarantee I won't reveal anything to any other media representative."

"And you'll agree to that Sue?" Joanne asks Sue Weissman.

Sue nodded. "I certainly will. And I think my editor will see the benefit in having exclusive rights to the full story."

"Can, can you really bring Skye home?" Joanne asks me.

That's a question I had been asking myself. *Can I? What if she doesn't want to come home?*

"I know I can find Skye. After that, there are no promises. If, for example, she's safe where she is and there are reasons why she doesn't want to return home, I need to consider that. Because she's a minor, she may not have a choice, but that won't be my decision alone. Either way, I can find her and she will have to be in touch with you. That I can guarantee."

"Why do you think she might not want to come home?" Joanne suddenly seems a little defiant. "Do you know something?"

"I know that she's safe and that she's alright. If that's the case, I'm trying to sort out why she won't come home, or at least be in touch. I'm not there yet.

Can I ask you a few questions Mrs Burrows?"

She nods. "Anything."

"You asked me earlier where Skye is. I didn't answer because I honestly don't know yet, but I believe she's not very far away and that she may even still be in Lismore. Assuming she's in Lismore, do you have any idea where she could be?"

Sue replies, "Roy, Lismore isn't that big. If we had any idea where Skye is we would've found her already. The police have visited all of the friends and ex-friends Joanne could think of and they can't find any trace of Skye. Also, they don't think any of these people are acting suspiciously."

"Mrs Burrows?" I ask.

"It's as Miss Weissman said. We gave the police the names and contact details of anyone and everyone we could think of, and I know the police have asked these kids if they could think of anywhere that Skye could be. So far there is no more information that I am aware of."

"I agree," Sue says. "I check daily. There's nothing."

I ponder over this for a few minutes, wondering if Joanne Burrows is telling the entire truth. I have trouble believing that a young girl would leave home if everything is nice and rosy. And, if there was some other reason, nothing to do with her home, why not be in touch at least? It just doesn't make sense to me and I can't help wondering if there's more to it.

But what? And I remember my spirit guide also seemed undecided on this issue.

"Mrs Burrows, Joanne, has anything happened at home recently which might've caused Skye to leave?"

There, I've asked what's probably one of the most difficult questions.

Joanne doesn't seem happy with the question. "What are you getting at? Why are you asking that?"

"Quite simple Joanne. I'm trying to help locate your daughter. To do that, I need to know all there is to know."

"Well the answer is no!" She says, rather abruptly, and defensively. "Nothing's happened that's different or unusual as far as I'm concerned. Our life is the same as always.

Anyway, where's that paper you want me to sign? I need to be at the doctors' in half an hour."

Sue goes to the computer and prints off some more copies of the revised agreement. She comes back with five pages. "If we three each sign all copies, I'll get my editor to sign them all and he can keep one, then I'll give you each a fully signed copy so we all have the same."

"What about the fifth one?" I wonder. "Why are we signing five and not four?"

"Call it insurance." Sue replies. "I'd like to get one to the General Manager of the Globe, so there can be no disputing what has been agreed. Not that I don't trust my editor, but positions change fairly frequently. If the GM is aware of the agreement, any new editor will be bound by the agreement."

"That sounds logical. "

It makes sense to me anyway.

"Mr Addams," Joanne asks. "Where do we go from here? I mean if we agree not to tell anyone, how can you question people, and that sort of thing?"

It's a good question, and I managed to give the issue some thought after Sue Weissman asked the same thing earlier.

"Joanne, your question is quite valid and our agreement does limit my investigation to some extent, but with the police, Paul and perhaps a few other people, I'll simply say that I'm still making up my mind and that I need a little more background information to help me do that."

Sue nods her head in agreement. "That should work. It sounds totally fine to me. After all, no-one would take on a case until they had all the facts and could see a way forward, would they?"

"Do you want me to organise something with Paul?" Joanne stands to leave.

"Not yet, thanks. I think I'd like to talk with the police first. I'll get back to you."

Joanne leaves with her copy of the agreement. She goes without saying any more. I think she looks confused, as if she's deep in thought, and I'm confused about her for some reason I can't quite put my finger on.

Sue looks at me, a quizzical look and a slight grin on her face. "You were pretty blunt with her. In fact you seem totally different to when we spoke yesterday, more direct, more confident, that sort of thing. Are you taking something?

I look at Sue and smile.

"Sue, yesterday I was surprised. I had no idea about the case, who Skye and Joanne Burrows are and what I could expect of myself. Plus, I was trying to come to grips with the fact you represent a local paper, and there was a degree of urgency on your part. Urgency sometimes makes me nervous.

Today I've had a chance to contact my, well, my guides. And from initial responses I know they will help. And we've negotiated an agreement that I think will be

87

beneficial, particularly to me because I'll be able to concentrate on the case. I mean concentrate on issues as they come up, without all and sundry looking over my shoulder every day to see what I'm doing and wondering why there are no updates in the daily press.

So yes, I'm more relaxed about it all, and it feels good."

"And me?" Sue has a strange look on her face. "How do you feel about me now?"

"In all honesty Sue, you seem much more relaxed today too. Less pushy, sorry but I think you know what I mean, and more cooperative. And I'm not sure why, but I feel we've established a better way forward."

"Fair enough, and I guess I know what you mean, I can be pretty focused at times.

Now, I've cancelled most of my commitments for today so I can be at your disposal. I had no idea if you were going to come on board, so it was going to be a day of trying to convince you if I had to, or helping you, depending on your decision.

"I would like to talk with one of the police officers who might be in charge of the case, if possible. And that Ken Wood too. Can that be arranged?"

"I'm sure neither will be a problem. If I'm there anyway." Sue says with a cheeky grin. "Do you want it to be now, today?"

"As soon as we can, I guess.

It's almost twelve now. Can you see what you can arrange for say two o'clock today? And perhaps we can have lunch somewhere first. That's if you don't mind being seen with an old man."

It was my turn to smile, probably with a funny grin on my face. I found the idea of having lunch with Sue interesting and a little amusing.

"And we can talk over tactics."

"Done! Just give me time to make a call or two."

Sue dials a number and walks around the room as she talks.

The final thing I hear her say is. "Around two? Great, we'll be there. And you'll try to make sure Ray Phipps is available? Perfect, thanks Ken.

Well, that's all fixed. Now where shall we go for lunch?"

She smiles and adds. "And by the way, you said something about me minding being seen with an old man, and the answer is no, of course I don't mind. But how do you feel about being seen around town with a woman with a bit of a reputation?"

It's my turn to smile again.

"I don't know anybody like that."

"Damn," Suzie says, as we walk to the car. "We let Joanne leave with her copy of the agreement. It hasn't been signed by my editor."

"I'm not sure it really matters Sue. The important agreement is between me and the paper, as far as publication anyway. Because she knows we each have a copy which she has signed, I think we're covered."

Chapter Eight

The café Sue chooses is a nice place that I'd been to before, and we sit at an outside table, in the sun. I've got my favourite cap on, a seven panelled one I picked up when I was holidaying in Puerto Rico a few years ago. Well, maybe ten years ago now. It's old and stained but it seems to fit me better than most others I've bought over the years.

Sue doesn't appear to mind that my cap looks a little shabby.

We order. I choose a light pasta dish, sort of heavy for a mid-day meal but I ask them to make it entrée size. Sue orders a chicken salad.

I need to clear up a few things with her before we meet the police.

"Sue, when we meet Ken Wood and the other guy, I may seem a little, well, let's say a little vague and non-committal, but I need to act that way.

I don't want them to think that I'm committed in any way and if they see me as being a doddery old fool, then, so be it. I find I often get more information that way."

"An interesting approach," Sue smiles. "But you're not a doddery old fool are you? You're far from it."

91

"I have my moments. But it's a good façade to hide behind and, believe me, it gets easier to play the part as I get older. It almost comes naturally at times."

"Ha!" Says Sue.

"Dad! What are you doing here?"

Suddenly Lisa is behind me. She's with two of her friends, Bella Lewis and Sharon Gould.

Bella, what sort of name is that I wonder? Is it from the Italian 'bella,' an abbreviation for something or even some sort of nick-name?

"Hi Lisa, Bella, Sharon. We're on our way to see the police. You know Sue Weissman I think?"

I'm trying to act pretty casual.

"Oh, yes we've met. Sorry, hi Sue." They all shake hands politely. "Does this mean you're taking the case dad?" Lisa seems a little put out, probably miffed because I haven't called to tell her my decision.

"No, just the opposite actually.

I've told Sue that I'm very much undecided and I'm worried about the calls we each received last night. She's offered to introduce me to Ken Wood, the police chief in Lismore and some people involved in the case. Sue seems to know most of them.

Hopefully they may be able to suggest who has been calling us and help put a stop to it."

I can just imagine Lisa saying '*I bet she does*' when I mentioned that Sue knew most of the police, but she doesn't.

"Oh, I see," Lisa replies. "That sounds like a good idea. I was really worried last night. And I still don't know how that Fletcher guy could've found my number."

"You're in the directory aren't you?" Sue asks calmly.

Lisa looks at Sue. I think she's going to respond, and possibly say something, but she doesn't. She ignores Sue's remark, which I thought was fairly logical actually, maybe just a bit sarcastic.

"Actually I think it's a great idea, you getting this business sorted out with the police, and thanks Sue for helping. And you won't forget about soccer tomorrow will you? I'll drop Michael off, but it would be a big help if you could bring him home."

To me it seems as though Lisa is trying hard to be polite, and positive, which is nice. I know she can be fairly judgemental at times.

I'm probably getting a little too cynical but I can't help wondering why Lisa doesn't stay at the game. I'm sure the younger kids would enjoy being out.

Maybe another coffee morning?

"No problem. I'll be there."

Actually I had sort of put the fact that it was Friday, and that the soccer match was the following day, totally out of my mind. But I know when I got home and read my notes I'll remember. I always seem to.

Lisa, Bella and Sharon move off, heading for a vacant table not far away.

"You got sprung mate." Sue says, winking. "Will it be a problem?

"Hell I don't know. But if becomes one, I really can't see why.

Lisa is very protective of me, over-protective in fact. She's probably in a bit of a quandary with me now. While she may not like the idea of me being with you, or anyone else for that matter, she must also see it's for a good reason. To sort out this Barry Fletcher business."

"And why wouldn't she like the idea of you being with me?" Sue asks. "What have I done, to her or anyone else?"

"As I said, I don't think she likes the idea of me being with any single lady, and not just you. By the way, are you single? I've never thought to ask before, sorry."

"Actually I am single," Sue replies. "I was married, for about eight years actually. James was killed in a car crash and I've never found anyone else. And I guess I've dedicated myself to my job ever since he died."

"Shit! I'm sorry, Sue." *I honestly had no idea what her marital situation was.*

"Poppa Roy, it was almost ten years ago now, but thanks."

Our meals arrive and we eat quietly. The pasta is great and the size of the serve is just right, enough to enjoy without making myself feel bloated.

When we finish, Sue asks. "Do you need to say anything to Lisa? I'll wait for you."

I shake my head. "No. we're fine. Let's go; but can we drive past Skye Burrows' home on the way please?"

"Sure, no problem." Sue says.

I smile and wave to Lisa. She and her friends wave back, and we walk to Sue's car. I can feel the three pairs of eyes following us.

"Guess I'll hear some more about this later." I mutter as we get into the car, not really addressing it to Sue, but she hears.

"I think you're old enough, and smart enough to handle it." Sue says, laughing.

She drives the car and I watch her. I like watching her. Her skirt, which looks reasonably demure when she is standing, has ridden up a little but she doesn't pull it down. *She has nice legs. I notice, as if for the first time.*

As I requested, Sue points out the Burrows house then turns a few corners and drives past a school.

"This is the school Skye went to." She says. "It's only a few streets from her home, probably not much more than a kilometre."

I make some comment, thanking her and she drives on.

We pull up in the police station car park.

"Wait a minute Roy." She says. "I just need to make myself irresistible."

She reaches for her hand-bag and opens the mirror in the back of the sun visor. Taking a tube of lip-stick and a brush from her bag, she touches up her lips, and brushes her hair. Then she puts her hand-bag to one side, undoes the first two buttons of her blouse and folds the sides back a little.

"You can be a saucy wench." I'm laughing a little.

"Hey mister, you have your ways and your façade, and I have mine. Let's hope they both get the results we need."

With that she opens the door and steps out of the car.

"Now! Our relationship is very formal." Sue looks serious.

"Of course. And it is, isn't it?"

Sue just gives me a big smile and leads the way up the stairs and into the police station.

"Sue Weissman and Roy Addams to see Ken Wood." Sue says to the young, uniformed officer behind the front counter. She leans on the counter and the officer blushes and seems to have trouble looking Sue in the face.

"Of course, please wait here." He says, then adds. "Sorry, but can you both please sign the visitors' book here?" He points to a book on the counter.

He disappears. Sue puts her name and details in the register and signs it and I do the same, entering ditto for the date, time and the person we're going to visit.

After a few minutes, the young officer opens a side door and beckons us to follow him. "Inspector Wood will see you now." He says.

Sue leads the way and I follow.

She knocks on a door at the end of the passage and pushes it open.

The man behind the desk stands and comes to greet us. He is tall and well dressed, in a suit and white shirt. He looks to be in his late thirties, perhaps early forties. His tie is loosened.

He takes Sue's outstretched hand in both of his.

"Miss Weissman. Lovely to see you again. How have you been?"

"I'm fine Inspector Wood," Sue says, taking back her hand. "And this is Roy Addams." She adds, by way of introduction.

"Mr Addams, Roy. Welcome. We've certainly heard a lot about you. In fact we've got quite a thick file on you, but all good."

"Thank you Mr Wood." I decide I'll stay on formal terms until and unless invited to do otherwise. "Then you have a huge advantage over me Mr Wood. I really don't know anything about you. In fact last time I was here there was someone else in this position."

"Ah yes. That would have been Leo Bryant.

He retired about a year ago and I transferred up from Grafton to take up the senior role.

Please, sit down." Wood says, moving back to his side of the desk.

Chapter Nine

"Mr Addams." Ken Wood opens up the discussion.

"Miss Weissman tells me that you've been asked personally by the family, to be involved in the search for Skye Burrows."

I nod.

"I don't know how much you know about Skye, or if you propose taking up their request. Perhaps it may be best if you clarify your position first."

No beating around the bush with him, I notice.

"I know very little actually, Inspector Wood. I've met Skye's mother, Joanne and I've driven past her home and the school she attended. That's about it I'm afraid.

And, at this stage I haven't decided if I want to be involved. I'm sure your men are quite competent and would have conducted investigations in all possible areas, as far as interviewing friends, teachers and that sort of thing.

So, honestly, unless something jumps out at me as a further area which should be addressed, I can't see that I can add anything new.

But it is an interesting case."

"Interesting? How so?" Wood asks.

"Well, I find it odd that Skye Burrows wasn't seen after she left home. From my scant knowledge of the area, there would've been a reasonably high number of people out and about at that specific time, especially with the high school and the primary school being so close together. And, apart from the students arriving at each school, there would've been teachers arriving and parents dropping their children off, a lot of people in total."

"You say that as if you have given that aspect a lot of thought, and have a theory." Wood is hoping for me to respond and he's looking at me as if he's trying to penetrate through to my brain.

"Yes and no. I think Skye either turned in the opposite direction from the two schools, or she went into a house or a car perhaps immediately after leaving home. Otherwise it is most likely she would have been seen. The third possibility of course is that she never left home.

Well, not then anyway. And, I think I remember Mrs Burrows saying she never actually saw Skye leave."

"Interesting!" Wood exclaims. "I admire your powers of observation and deduction even after such a brief exposure to the case. And you're right of course, in that if she had followed her normal routine of getting to school, we believe she should have been seen. There are almost one and a half thousand students in the two schools, not to mention the teachers and parents, as you've said.

I'm impressed.

What else have you concluded?" Wood appears interested and sits forward in his chair.

"Not a lot, believe me. Mainly because I don't know if I'm interested, although,"

I stop intentionally, wanting to add a pregnant pause.

"Although, Mr Addams?" Sue prompts. She has no idea what more I might share with Ken Wood.

"Well, and these are purely personal opinions. I believe Skye is alive and not far from her home. But I don't think she's your typical runaway, nor that she's been abducted. I believe she left home for a specific reason and doesn't want to be found. To me this would suggest she doesn't want to return home, not yet anyway."

"That sounds like a fairly definite deduction on your part Mr Addams."

Ken Wood leans back in his chair. He looks genuinely surprised. "And I suppose you have some bases for coming to these conclusions."

"Well no, not really. My guess is that your people will have checked buses, trains, cameras in airports and perhaps even on the highways, but that you've probably discovered nothing conclusive. Using what I call an obvious non-obvious therefore, I've concluded that she probably didn't leave Lismore at all. Perhaps I'm wrong but I haven't heard of any information confirming that she did.

And you've probably had people scouring parks, bush lands and that sort of thing but without finding any clues, nothing to suggest that foul play may have been involved. Therefore I conclude it probably wasn't. Again, it was perhaps considered likely initially but there is really no evidence. To me, that makes it another obvious non-obvious, if that makes sense. I think she is safe and well, and somewhere close by."

"Mr Addams," Sue says, looking genuinely surprised, although she should've known my basic conclusions already. "If what you say is true, Skye Burrows is alive and perfectly well."

"Perhaps Miss Weissman, perhaps." I smile and nod. "But remember, I've only been thinking about this case for just over twenty-four hours. Perhaps I'm right in thinking she never left Lismore, and I think I am. But I could be totally wrong on every other point. She may have left home willingly enough but could now be here somewhere, being held against her will, a prisoner.

There are so many variables and possibilities. And remember, I'm an old man, with a lot of time to think and postulate. So a lot of my suggestions are hunches at best, based on what little I know."

"And what is your current thought as to getting involved Mr Addams?" Ken Wood asks.

I had been waiting for this question. It gives me a lead-in to air my supposed misgivings.

"Inspector Wood, as much as the case is intriguing to some degree, and it would be good to help Joanne Burrows, I have reservations.

A huge one is this Barry Fletcher business. Not only did he call me, as Miss Weissman has no doubt told you, but he also called my daughter, Lisa."

"I wasn't aware of that Mr Addams. I'm sorry." He says.

I continue. "Whoever it was that called didn't actually threaten me, or Lisa for that matter, but it worries me that asking me not to get involved may only be the first step.

104

Do you have any idea who it may be?"

"Frankly, no, I have no idea." Ken replies. "We've verified that it's definitely not anyone from the department. Sydney confirms there's one Barry Fletcher currently employed but he's stationed in Wentworth, a long way from here. So we're concluding either this guy's not a police officer or his name isn't Barry Fletcher, or it may be both of course.

Is this why you're not inclined to get involved?" Ken asks.

"It's certainly one reason. Maybe the most important one, especially as it now involves my family, but there are others."

"Go on." He says.

"Well, I'm also in the process of gathering information so I can write a memoir, about my life, the jobs I did when I was working and the cases I've been involved in since I retired. I have most of the records together and now I'm reviewing and editing everything and arranging items chronologically. It takes a lot of time and my getting involved in anything else would interrupt the logical flow of that process."

I think I can see a slight smirk on Sue's face. She knows the memoir bit is just a smoke screen.

"Another point, and this may be peculiar to this case. So far, I can't see a way forward that your people may not have covered already. Not yet anyway. Nothing jumps out at me as an avenue to investigate further.

For example, I've met Joanne Burrows several times and, to a great extent anyway, she acts like I would expect a grieving mother to act. But there's something else. I can't put my finger on it, but something about her doesn't seem quite real, not quite honest, if that makes sense.

I'm sure your expert investigators are looking into it, but I just don't have the expertise nor the authority to investigate her further."

I see Ken Wood making notes as I speak.

That's interesting. Hopefully they will investigate Joanne a little.

"Anything else?" Ken asks.

"Well there's Paul, Joanne's partner. I know you've had him in the station a few times and I assume, and all I can do at the moment is assume, that he may be, or may have been, a suspect of sorts.

I haven't met him, but if I were to take on the case I think I'd like to. But again, I don't have access to whatever criminal history he may have, nor the authority to demand he answer questions, if he should choose to not do so.

Unfortunately, I'm not too good in cases where things are dependent on one or two individuals, rather than just facts. It leaves me no real direction to take."

"But hang on a minute." Ken says. "I've read your history and I know that a lot of the cases you've helped solve previously have been similar, some almost identical. What's so different about this one?"

He's taken my bait.

"Apart from the fact that I'm getting older and, well, let's just say older. You'll find that in all similar cases I've been asked to be involved by the police department, and given access to all records, sat in on interviews and that sort of thing. That's not the situation here, and consequently I would be working blindly, probably covering ground that your men might have covered a hundred times already. It's not the same."

I let that sink in. I have no idea how Ken might react but what I said is true, well, most of it. On previous cases which were similar, Inspector Bryant would call me when the missing person's report, or whatever it was, was lodged, and we'd confer right from the start.

Ken Wood doesn't say anything for a few moments and I assume he is weighing up what I said.

Although it isn't exactly true that I was involved in every case from the very outset, he seems to have accepted what I have said as fact.

After a pause of almost a full minute, he says. "So, if I understand you correctly, you want access to our records and to sit in on our investigation. Is that about right?"

"Not at all. There's still the matter of Barry Fletcher to think about, and my memoir. Those are the main reasons. The others are just me explaining a few differences, and reasons why my involvement would be, well, handicapped, I guess is the right word."

"I understand."

That's what Ken Wood says, but I'm not sure he does. I'm not sure I do either actually. Most of what I said was a product of my imagination, although Leo Bryant and I did have a very good rapport. And I thought it was something Wood couldn't easily verify.

"The Barry Fletcher thing has put you off because of the potential threat to you and your family. I understand and appreciate that's a major concern."

I just nod and try to look concerned.

"And you seem to be at a crucial stage in preparing a memoir of your life, which is keeping you busy?"

I nod again.

Actually I've shuffled heaps of papers and case notes about a few times but I'm no closer to putting together a memoir now than I was when my wife was alive. But there's no way he can verify that either.

"Can I ask a couple of questions?" Sue asks.

Ken Wood smiles. "Of course Sue."

"I was told that Ray Phipps would be here this afternoon as well. Is there any development? Some reason he isn't here?"

"Well yes, perhaps," Ken seems a little cagey. "We had a call just after twelve that a girl matching Skye's description was seen in the Lismore Square Shopping Centre. Ray and a few of his team headed over to investigate. But I thought they would've been back by now, and no, I haven't heard anything from them."

"Okay, I did wonder. Thought you were just keeping us all to yourself." Sue smiles.

"My other question concerns Paul." Sue continues. "I know you've had him in the station a few times. I've only met him once but he seems a bit odd to me, not shifty, just different. I can't really suggest what it is but it almost seems to me as though he has something to hide, if that makes sense.

I guess he just seems odd to me. How did he check out? If I can ask that sort of question?"

I think she's fairly game, asking such a direct question, but I'm also intrigued about Paul Burrows.

"You can ask." Ken Wood says. "But knowing you're a reporter and that anything I say might appear in tomorrow's Globe, you'll appreciate that, apart from the usual confidentiality aspects, I can't say much."

"Forget the bloody paper Ken!" Sue says, probably a little more forcefully than necessary.

"This is just the three of us chatting and you know I always clear things with you before going to print. If I didn't, my job would be on the line."

"Yes. Sorry Sue," Ken says. "I realize that and yes, you have always respected my position.

110

Okay, so what can I tell you? We also considered Paul to be a little different, as you suggest. And he did appear as if he was hiding something.

We weren't sure what, if anything, so we brought him in a few times. Without giving too much away, we came to the conclusion that he's just a loner and that his background explains his demeanour to a large extent. And I'm not about to explain that in detail, but we're generally convinced he's not involved."

"Only generally convinced?" Sue asks.

"Well yes, generally. There are still a few doubting Thomases on the team, but the general consensus is he's okay. And that's my opinion too by the way, for what it's worth."

"Okay, thanks Ken. Humour me please. Do you think Paul could be Barry Fletcher? From what you know of him, is it the type of thing you could see him doing?"

Ken looks a little inquisitive, as if he's weighing it over, or analysing my question somehow. He shakes his head.

"No. I really don't think so, Mr Addams," he replies after a few moments. "I don't see him as the type of person who would come out and do something like that. He's very much an introvert and I just don't see him playing that sort of role."

"Okay, thanks, Inspector Wood. Just a thought."

"And possibly a good one. But I honestly don't think it's him." Ken says. "And if you talk to him yourself I'd value your opinion."

I get up. I've heard enough and I don't think Ken Wood is willing, or able, to tell us anything new.

"Thanks Inspector Wood," I hold out my hand for him to shake. "If I decide to get seriously involved in the case, or if I hear from this Fletcher guy again, I'll be in touch."

Sue hadn't quite finished. "Just one more point Ken. Putting on my Globe hat for a moment, sorry. Can I quote you about the suspected sighting of Skye Burrows in the Square Shopping Centre today?"

"Yes, I guess you can Sue. But why don't you wait. I'll give you a call when Ray Phipps comes back, then you'll have the most up to date information. And I promise I'll call you before I let anyone put out a general announcement."

"Thanks Ken." Sue says, standing and holding out her hand for him to shake. "We'll talk later."

I wasn't sure exactly what the 'talk later' meant but I didn't really care. From the sound of it, Sue is going to get an exclusive story, which is good, for her and her paper.

We leave the station and make our way to Sue's car. She asks if I mind waiting for a few minutes before she starts the car. I don't mind of course. I'm in no hurry.

Sue takes out her telephone and calls someone. I assume it's her editor.

"Frank? Frank listen!" Frank was probably trying to say something. "I'm just leaving the police station.

Apparently there was a suspected sighting of Skye Burrows, or someone who looks a lot like her in the Lismore Square Shopping Centre today. Just a few hours ago actually. We can print that, on the authority of Inspector Wood but I'm also going to get more details once his team returns to the station. Yes, that's right, I'm getting an exclusive, before any general announcement. So set up space for an article and how long it ends up will depend on what details I get. I suggest we could lead on page one and perhaps follow up with detail on another page, so we can keep the page one bit as a featured headline.

Why me and us? Don't ask. You should know the answer by now Frank. Because I'm good at what I do."

"Men!" Sue says, after she finishes the call. "When they think I'm not doing my job well, it's because I'm a woman. But when I do and I'm offered an exclusive, it's also just because I'm a woman. I can't win."

I laugh.

I know exactly what she means, and that she's right but there's not much I can add. We men are pretty hopeless really. When a female political leader cries at some crisis or other, she's branded as weak. If she doesn't cry, or show some similar emotion, she's branded as being hard and heartless. I totally understand Sue's frustration.

She drives.

When we pull up at my house, there's another car parked in front. It's Lisa's and she's sitting in it, with her mobile phone to her ear. I'm not sure if she's talking or perhaps trying to call me. But I left my mobile phone inside anyway. Basically, I hate the things. Any privacy we had is being eroded bit by bit and the expectation that we should always be accessible takes out a huge chunk.

"Let's give her something to gossip about." Sue unfastens her seat belt, leans over to my side and kisses me on the cheek. "There. That should do it."

"Off you go, and let me know what happens." Sue says, with a cheeky grin. "Oh, and if you have any additional revelations about the case of course."

I think I'm blushing a little when I get out of the car. Not really embarrassed, more surprised.

Sue drives off and I wave her goodbye then walk over to Lisa's car.

Lisa gets out, and locks her car, then turns to me. "What have you been up to dad? What was that about?"

"Just Sue's way of saying goodbye I guess. Come on, let's go inside. I'll tell you about our visit to the police station. Also some news you won't hear about officially until later today or tomorrow morning."

That was really just by way of a subject changer, but it seemed to work.

"Why, what's happened?" Lisa asks as we walk to the front door. "Is it something to do with Skye Burrows?"

I unlock the door, making a fuss of opening the deadlock so she notices I'm using it.

Once inside, I suggest we sit down. "Give me a minute. It's been a long day."

Lisa sits patiently. I'm sure she would love to ask again but she doesn't.

"Around lunch time today, well, when we were having lunch I guess, there was a reported sighting of Skye Burrows, at the Lismore Square Shopping Centre. The officer in charge, a guy named Ray Phipps and members of his team went to the Centre to investigate.

Phipps was supposed to be in the meeting with us but he was still out of the office, so we only saw the boss, Inspector Ken Wood. Ken took Inspector Bryant's place when he retired. Do you remember Bryant? You met him a few times."

"Forget the Inspectors damn it." Lisa is impatient. "Was it Skye Burrows or not?"

"Oh sorry. We don't actually know yet. As I said, Phipps wasn't in the station. He and his team hadn't returned, or reported in, by the time we left, but Inspector Wood said he'll call Sue as soon as they do, and give her an exclusive."

"She must have impressed him." Lisa mutters. "Well, what else happened?"

"We had a good visit with Inspector Wood actually. He seems quite good. A lot younger than Bryant but I guess that's progress. Bryant had been there a long time."

"Dad! What happened?"

"Oh sorry Lisa. I explained the Barry Fletcher business and said I'm worried about getting involved, even though there haven't been any threats as such. As I told Ken Wood, *who knows what might happen next?'*

Then there's the matter of my memoir. I've been working on it off and on, and I told him I'd like to keep going and get it finished while the grey matter is still functioning reasonably well, and I can still remember things.

I also pointed out that things were different when Bryant was the boss. I was usually consulted much earlier by the police, and could sit in on interviews and that sort of thing. But things are different now."

"So you're not taking on the case? I'm glad. The Fletcher thing certainly worried me. Anything else?"

"Well yes, I guess so. They honestly have no idea who this Barry Fletcher might be, which is a bit of a worry. There is actually a Barry Fletcher in the police force but he's stationed in Wentworth or somewhere like that, so Ken is satisfied it's not him. Either Fletcher isn't a policeman or it's a false name. Either of those or both, we agreed were possible.

Oh, and we discussed Paul, Joanne's partner. Sue's met him and said she thought he seemed a bit odd. I think that

117

was how she put it anyway, different or odd, I'm not sure of the exact words she used.

Anyway, Ken Wood agreed that Paul comes across as a bit of a loner but the police checked out his background and Wood says there are reasons Paul seems different, but he wouldn't elaborate. And the police are convinced Paul is not involved in Skye's disappearance. I also asked Wood if he thought Paul could be our Barry Fletcher, but he said no, he didn't believe so."

"You've certainly had a busy day dad. What are you going to do now?"

"I think I'll watch television for a while, see the early news, have a bite to eat and then an early night. I need to be up early in the morning and out on the soccer pitch."

"As I said before, I'll drop Michael off." Lisa says. "His match kicks off some time after eight thirty, so if you can be there around then that'll be great. And bring him home of course.

Oh, and he may want to stop and watch the next game if there is one. But that's totally up to you. Whatever you can manage. And thank you."

With that she kisses me on the cheek. *Two kisses today.* Lisa lets herself out the front door.

118

I have no intention of watching television. There's too much on my mind.

Chapter Ten

I sit with my blank writing pad in front of me. It's still reasonably early so I decide to ask a lot of questions, and to try to cover all the areas I have doubts about. And there are a lot.

Even Sue. *Can I trust her?* My last answers told me not to trust anyone, *what about Ken Wood or even Lisa. And of course, what about Joanne and Paul? Can I trust them?* I really have no idea but I decide I need to find out.

I use a clean sheet and write out my questions.

Should I trust Sue Weissman?

Can I believe Sue Weissman?

Should I trust Inspector Ken Wood?

Should I trust Lisa, my daughter?

Should I trust Joanne Burrows?

Can I believe Joanne Burrows?

Should I trust Paul, Joanne's partner?

Should I trust Skye Burrows?

That probably covers all the trust issues, I can think of, and I put that sheet to one side.

I've learnt from past experience that three sheets of paper side by side are all that I seem to be able to work on at the same time, so I intend to limit myself to three sheets now.

The most pressing thing preventing me from getting too excited about the case is this character Barry Fletcher, so I devote a sheet to him.

Is the man's name really Barry Fletcher?

Do I know him?

What is his real name?

Is he a police officer?

Is he in Lismore?

Has he anything to do with Skye Burrows?

Is he involved in her disappearance?

Is he involved in some way with any of the people in this case?

Which person is he involved with?

I decide that if I get answers to most of these questions, I might have a better idea of what's going on.

My third sheet I devote to questions about Skye Burrows herself. After all, while I think I know a lot, really I know nothing about where she might actually be, or why she isn't home with her family.

Where is Skye Burrows?

Is she free to return home if she wants to?

Is someone holding her against her will?

Is she with someone who is protecting her?

Did she leave home willingly?

Does she want to return home?

If she doesn't want to return home, why not?

Does she have a problem with her mother?

Does she have a problem with Paul, her step-father?

I read through the questions.

I know I have asked much the same ones before but I decide I need to ask them again, if only to verify what I already think are the answers.

It's almost six. I want to know if the police found anything new when they went to the Square Shopping Centre earlier, so I call Sue Weissman. Even though Ken Wood gave me his business card, I don't feel good about calling him.

"Sue? Hi Sue. Sorry for calling you after hours again but I just wonder if you've had any feedback about the possible sighting at the Square today?"

"Hi Poppa Roy. Yes and no.

The two women who reported the sighting work in one of the shops and they are adamant it was her. The police showed them several photographs and they insisted it was

122

Skye, and that she was with another girl, or possibly a young woman. They think the other person was about twenty, and they've given the police a reasonably good description of her.

Because the two girls both wore hooded jackets, hoodies I think the kids call them, the women only partially saw their faces really, except for an instant when the Skye character pushed her hood back and brushed her hair off of her forehead, then pulled the hood back in place.

I'm actually in the Globe office now, just finalizing a story for tomorrow's issue. Do you get the paper?"

"No Sue. Sorry, but I avoid the local papers. In fact I don't read any paper in hard copy. I just look at news items on the internet occasionally."

"Why not read my paper?" She sounded a bit put out, but I wasn't sure if she was serious, or just teasing me.

"Unfortunately, and don't get me wrong Sue, I appreciate you probably represent the area well. But I find local papers appear to have too much local content, if that makes sense, and too many articles, letters and that sort of thing appear to highlight people with vested interests or personal axes to grind. Rather than what I would regard as being real news.

Sorry, it's just my opinion."

"Fair enough. We all have our opinions and, to some extent, I agree with you, some of the time anyway, but it's what gets us our circulation. Local people seem to like to read about local issues and local opinions."

"What about CCTV Sue? Surely there are a lot of cameras in the Square, in the malls and in the car park."

"Yes, of course." She says. "Sorry I should have mentioned them. Ken said his men checked everything they could and there is vision of two females wearing grey hoodies on a few of the cameras, but none which shows their faces clearly. He actually emailed me a few still shots taken from the TV's and I'm including one in my article.

There is something strange though. Although they appeared on four or five of the cameras in the mall, the cameras in the car park didn't pick them up at all.

I'm not sure if you know the Square very well but the entrances are from the car park, so it's odd."

"If my memory is right, and that is sometimes a big *if.* I get confused about which shopping centre is which sometimes. Isn't there an entrance through some other shops, an electrical place and a shop which sells motoring bits and pieces?"

"Hey! You're right." Sue says. "Absolutely! And I assume there are cameras in that small mall between the two groups of shops, and in the other shops. I wonder if the police checked those? I'll find out.

And another thing, Poppa Roy. It looks like you could be spot on as far as Skye still being in Lismore. And she may be here of her own free will just as you thought.

I'm impressed. More than I was I mean of course. I was impressed anyway, but now? Wow! Doubly so."

"Thank you Miss Sue."

I like the fact that she actually believes me.

"But unless the sighting can be confirmed somehow, it is still only a sighting of someone who could be Skye Burrows. We shouldn't lose sight of that and we need to keep things in perspective."

"You're right of course. But we're going to make it our lead story anyway. It's what sells papers I'm afraid."

"Your poetic licence or whatever the newspaper equivalent is I guess. I might just buy a copy of the Globe in the morning. It will give me something to read at the soccer game."

"And what are you doing tonight Poppa Roy? It's Friday night. Are you planning a big night out on the town?"

I know she's just stirring me up.

"Actually I am about to disconnect this blasted telephone and try to lose myself and get some more answers. A few things worry me but mainly this Barry Fletcher thing, and if we can believe and trust Joanne Burrows.

For some reason something about her just doesn't ring true. I wish I knew what it is."

"And here I was wondering if you might be thinking about me, instead of Joanne. Oh well, that's the story of my life."

I think she's joking, teasing me. But I can't really tell, so I decide to play along with her a little.

I try to use my most serious voice. "The case first, Miss Weissman, the case first."

Sue laughs. "Good for you, Poppa Roy. Now I need to run and get this article to bed. Good night and sweet dreams. Of who-ever the lucky lady is."

With that, she ends the call.

I sit there for a few moments giving Sue too much of my mind than I probably should.

I shake my head, unplug the telephone at the wall and switch on my computer.

Chapter Eleven

My computer screen opens to the usual desktop. I double click on the mantras icon and select my favourite.

Before I attempt to lose myself, I tape the three sheets of paper on to the desk and place two pens on them.

I look over the mantra. I sometimes wonder if I should change my preferred mantra but it seems to work for me so I haven't bothered too much. It's just a notion in the back of my mind somewhere.

Concentrating on the mantra I change my routine. I look only at the angles, counting and memorising how many right angles I can see, then how many acute angles. Then I look for and count the obtuse angles.

I try to visualize what the mantra would look like if the colours were reversed. I stare at a corner only and the colours merge, then seem to settle out differently.

o0o

I look at the clock on the screen. It is just after eight thirty and I realize that my mind has been somewhere else for about two hours. For some reason, about two hours seems to be the time I'm usually somewhere else.

127

I look at the three sheets of paper stuck to the desk. There's writing on them, as I hoped there would be. In all honesty there usually is writing but it doesn't always make sense. Well, not to me anyway.

As often happens, I'm awe-struck by the simple way spirit writing, magic writing or whatever it is, seems to work.

And I wonder why more people don't use it. Or is it just me? Is it some kind of special gift? They say to never look a gift-horse in the mouth, so I don't really question why I have the gift. But I do question why other people don't seem to have it. Perhaps not many people try.

Another aspect which has bothered me more lately is the question of which spirits may be providing the answers. If in fact they are provided by external forces. I trust the answers I receive, and generally act on them.

But what if there are malevolent spirits as well? And what if answers start coming from them?

Then my answers could be totally false and whatever action I take as a result could be wrong. I decide, as I always do, that I shouldn't spend time worrying about something I don't really understand, and that I should just be happy that the answers I receive seem reasonable. *So far anyway*, a little bit of my mind suggests.

I switch on the desk light and study the sheets of paper.

Should I trust Sue Weissman?

YES

This reply is clear, Sue can be trusted!

Can I believe Sue Weissman?

YES

Again, I am glad the answer in relation to Sue is positive.

Should I trust Inspector Ken Wood?

?? NO

An interesting answer. I assume this may be because he is limited in how much truth he can tell me. But I'm not sure.

Should I trust Lisa, my daughter?

??YES

I wonder why the question marks. Why the doubt? I know Lisa sometimes says things she thinks are for my own good, my own well-being. Maybe that's the reason for some hesitation.

Should I trust Joanne Burrows?

NO!

Can I believe Joanne Burrows?

NO!

Both of these support my hunch that Joanne may have something she's not telling us. That she's possibly hiding something.

Should I trust Paul, Joanne's partner?

YES

That confirms the impression of Paul the police have seems correct.

Should I trust Skye Burrows?

??YES

The answer is a relief. I had wondered what would happen if I found her but couldn't believe or trust her. It would've created a huge problem for me, knowing what to do next.

I look through the answers on the first page, and try to make sense of some of the words written over the paper, not directly under the questions.

The only words which sort of make a sentence are

KEN WOOD IS NOT!

This confuses me a little. *He's not what?* I wonder.

I decide it doesn't matter. I've been told he can't be trusted anyway.

I look at the answers on my second sheet.

Is the man's name really Barry Fletcher?

NO!!!

Do I know him?

NO

What is his real name?

?????

Is he a police officer?

NO

So I now know he's not a police officer and that his name isn't Barry Fletcher. *Not much more than I thought was the case already.*

Is he in Lismore?

YES??

Again the question marks. *I wonder if that means he comes and goes?* Maybe he travels a lot.

Has he anything to do with Skye Burrows?

????NO????

Is he involved in her disappearance?

NO

131

Is he involved in some way with any of the people in this case?

???YES!!!

This, I read, to be a definite *yes* but only after some hesitation. I can't figure out why. *He is or he isn't involved in some way.*

Which person is he involved with?

???????

No definite answer. I'm disappointed. I had hoped this could be an easy way to solve the riddle of who he is. Then I realize that he may be involved with some or many, of the people, so perhaps there can't be a straight answer.

Where is Skye Burrows?

CLOSE

This answer is the same as the one I got last time I asked that question. It reinforces what I already believed to be the case. Skye is alive and in Lismore somewhere.

Is she free to return home if she wants to?

YES

Is someone holding her against her will?

NO

Is she with someone who is protecting her?

132

YES

Did she leave home willingly?

YES

Does she want to return home?

NO

If she doesn't want to return home, why not?

????????????

Does she have a problem with her mother?

????YES????

Does she have a problem with Paul, her step-father?

NO

I study these answers. Some are very definite and specific, others are vague or non-committal, such as the one about Skye's mother.

If nothing else, my *mumbo jumbo* reinforces my thought that Joanne Burrows is hiding something, *but what?*

I look at the other writing on the second and third pages. Not much of it makes sense, but then I notice the words **POOR PAUL** amongst a jumble of other letters, and wonder what it could mean.

Why poor Paul?

I assume this doesn't mean *poor* in the financial sense, and I wonder what could've been done to him. *Why would they refer to him as 'poor Paul?'*

Then another word jumps out at me from the jumble of letters. To me it looks like **CHRIS.** Unfortunately the letters either side don't make any sense and I can't form any words from them. *Who is Chris?* I wonder. *Is it a Christopher or perhaps a Christine, or even something else?*

I try to line up the 'Chris' with all of my questions but that doesn't seem to work. It's on the second sheet where I asked about Barry Fletcher. Then my old grey matter has an idea.

Could Chris be the real name of this Barry Fletcher? Or am I just assuming that because it suits me?

There's no definite correlation on the page, just me doing some creative imagining.

I see some other letters which could be another new name. **JA   NET.** There is a space between the letters. But maybe my hand slipped or caught on something. I really have no idea, but I think that perhaps the letters are meant to make up a name; *Janet.*

But who is Janet?   And where does Janet come into this mystery?

I write myself a summary of what I think the answers mean and add the names Chris and Janet, with plenty of question marks. If I'm to get any further with this investigation I need to know who they, Chris and Janet could be.

I look at the clock, almost nine pm. *Should I call Sue? Might she know?*

I decide it's probably not a good idea.

If she knew the names of anyone she thought had any relevance to the case, she would have mentioned them, wouldn't she?

If the responses can be believed, I can trust Sue so yes, I decide, *she would have told me.*

I switch off my computer. Time for bed I decide. Soccer in the morning.

I plug my telephone back into the wall socket and notice there are two missed calls registered. One is from Sue Weissman, and it came through forty minutes earlier, and the other is from an 'Unknown Number. *That could've been anyone* so I ignore it.

I decide that returning Sue's call would not be as bad as calling her out of the blue so I dial her number. But I don't plan to mention the two *new* names.

135

"Sue, oh hi. Sorry but I was somewhere else when you called, well, in my mind anyway. Do we have some more news?"

I assume she may have more news from the police.

"Hi Poppa Roy. I was a bit worried when you didn't answer and I've been wondering if I should drive over to make sure you're alright. Thanks for calling back.

I've had a couple of calls. One from Inspector Wood and the other from that man who calls himself Barry Fletcher. It was a funny voice though, it sounded very muffled. As if he was talking into a handkerchief or something. Was it the same with you?"

"Exactly the same. As if he was trying to disguise his voice for some reason. What did he say?"

"It was odd really. He introduced himself and said he was from the Missing Persons branch of the police, which I know is not true of course. Then he asked me if you're involved in the Skye Burrows investigation.

I told him that you weren't involved and that, because of calls you and your family had received, it was unlikely that you would become involved."

"That sounds perfect." *I'm impressed. It's basically what we had told Ken Wood.* "What did he say?"

"Nothing. He just hung up. Which is a shame, because I thought if he had kept talking I may have been able to work out who he is."

Sue really did sound disappointed.

"And the call from the police?"

"Ken called about fifteen minutes after the other guy. Acting on our suggestion, they reviewed whatever CCTV tapes they hadn't looked at before, including one in the mall section leading out to the electronics shop. Sure enough it shows two females in jeans and grey hoodies, walking from the main mall into the smaller one. But the police couldn't pick them up on any other camera. Not yet anyway, but they're still checking. Ken said one of the problems is some of the cameras are dummies, just there to dissuade shop-lifters and that sort of thing, and it seems there was no tape in some of the others. I'm not sure how those things work, but I assume if there's no tape in them, people can still monitor movement by looking at a screen somewhere, but there's no permanent record.

Looks like you were right again though Poppa Roy. They probably went out that way and that's why none of the cameras in the car park picked them up."

"Did Inspector Wood say anything else?"

137

"Well, apart from trying to chat me up, as he always does, no, not really. When I told him about Barry Fletcher calling, he sounded concerned. But I assured him that I was alright and that there were no threats, nothing like that."

Basically thinking out loud I said, "whoever this man is, he obviously knows a lot. He knows you are somehow involved, for example, and he's managed to get Lisa's number from somewhere. I wonder who he is really, and why he doesn't want me involved. Could he be a police officer who doesn't want me interfering in what he sees as their case, or is it something more sinister?"

Sue agrees. "It is odd. Calling you may not be an unusual thing to do but why Lisa and why me? I'm not your keeper."

"No Sue. You're not, and neither is Lisa.

Okay Miss Sue. It's been a long day and honestly I'm a bit drained. Also I've got to be out on the soccer pitch around eight thirty, but I want to do some more research first, so good night to you."

"Good night to you again, Poppa Roy. Sleep well."

We finish the call.

I think about what Sue had said, especially about Ken Wood trying to chat her up. An occupational hazard I guess.

138

If she dresses and acts sexily, men are bound to take that as an invitation, aren't they? I certainly think so.

I remember back to a time I was working on a job in West Africa. My twenty four year old South African Office Administrator, Marika, used to play up a little when she went to see the government or company officials, to get driving permits, gate passes and that sort of thing.

Her 'playing up' was limited to leaving a few buttons of her work shirt undone. I suggested to her, a single white female, that she was playing a dangerous game in what was very obviously a black man's country. She said she didn't think so, but later she confided in me that one of the black office supervisors had somehow got hold of her private telephone number and was calling her after hours at home. She asked for my help to stop him.

It put me in a difficult situation but, as the Project Manager and the number one company representative on site, I had to handle it. I went to see the guy concerned and explained that while she was a pretty girl, and sexy, she was engaged to be married. And that her fiancé worked for the same mining company in South Africa. Also that if her fiancé found out about the calls, I had no doubt he would go straight to this guy's boss. I said that while I had no idea what the outcome might be, I didn't think that his boss or the boss's boss, could afford to take the harassment of female customers lightly.

The office guy protested of course, that it wasn't harassment and he meant no harm.

I assured him that I believed him, but it wasn't what I thought that mattered. It was more a question of what the bosses might think, and that would probably depend on what Marika said.

I also promised if he stopped calling, I would make sure that neither she nor I would say or do anymore about it, and the issue would go away.

According to Marika, he didn't call again and, interestingly, when she needed his cooperation after that she got it immediately, and without the need to undo any buttons. My warning that it might be taken further appeared to have worked, and we received our permits and licenses more promptly than we ever had before.

Chapter Twelve

It's Saturday morning, and I wake a little tired after a restless night.

I had gone to bed with my mind churning over names, Skye, Joanne, Chris, Paul and Janet.

Where do they all fit? Do they fit together in some way?

I appreciated that finding and talking to Skye Burrows was undoubtably the key to finding out everything. My mind was full of *where is she? Where is she? Where is she?* The question tormented me as I dropped off to sleep. But of course there were no answers, not as I finally fell asleep, nor when I woke this morning.

Coffee! I must have coffee in the mornings.

Then I remember something. Damn, I should have remembered it before. I'm slipping.

Joanne promised me a list of all Skye's friends, and ex-friends. If I have that list, perhaps I can work out who *Chris* and *Janet* are. Possibly a long shot, but worth a try.

The clock shows me it's only seven thirty and I decide it's too early to call either Sue or Joanne. I have to be at the soccer ground around eight thirty, and it's only ten minutes' drive.

I'll call Sue at around eight fifteen, and I should still be at the game on time.

I busy myself getting ready. It looks like it's going to be a great day so I wear a pair of thin trousers and a summer shirt. But I go back into the bedroom and get a light cardigan, *just in case*.

At eight fifteen exactly I call Sue Weissman. I think I'll get more cooperation from Sue than from Joanne, and the guides have told me that Sue can be trusted, whereas Joanne can't.

"Hello! Good morning Poppa Roy," Sue answers, sounding a little husky, and nice. "To what do I owe this pleasure? It's pretty early and I'm still in bed."

"Still in bed?" I joke. "Almost half the day's gone."

"A girl needs her beauty sleep you know, especially when she's not so much of a girl any longer."

I can sense the smile in her voice. She sounds cute.

"Sorry Sue. I'm heading off to the soccer field in a few minutes. Do you want me to call you back later?"

"No. It's alright, I'm wide awake now. And what can I do for you this morning, or did you just miss me?"

142

I'm tempted to say something cute and suggestive, but it's not really my style. Well, it hasn't been for a lot of years, so I let it go.

"Sorry again Sue. I'll make it quick and you can turn over and drop off to sleep again.

Remember when we first spoke about Skye? I said I would need a list of all her friends, including ex-boyfriends, the girl she had problems with at school, all the names and contact details. And Joanne said she would get a list together for me, the same as she had done for the police.

Well, I sort of need that list as soon as possible. I have some new names which don't mean anything to me. The list might help."

"Are you going to tell me the names? I may recognise them."

I'm undecided. I've been told I can trust Sue, and I think I do, I ponder this.

"Don't, if you feel you can't, or shouldn't. It's up to you Roy."

"Sorry Sue, I was lost for a moment or two, thinking I should share them with you but realising how vague they really are."

143

This was a little white lie of course, with only some small element of truth.

My mind had also flickered on the subject of Skye's father. Joanne's ex-husband, Skye's real father was named *Jan*. But not *Janet*, not even close. Besides, being Dutch, he would have been called *Yan*, not *Jan*, anyway, by anyone who knew him.

"Yes, I trust you Sue, and I don't mind telling you. The names are *Chris*, and I have no idea if that's a Christine or a Christopher, or maybe even a derivation of some other name, I suppose, and *Janet*. But that could possibly be Jeanette or something similar. Do those mean anything to you?"

"Not off-hand I'm afraid. No surnames I suppose?"

"Afraid not Sue. And as they appeared to me on different sheets of answers, I don't think they are one and the same person, but I could be totally wrong of course."

I look at the time. We've been talking for nearly ten minutes and it's almost eight twenty-five.

"Sorry Sue but I must go. I need to be at the soccer ground about eight thirty. Can you see if you can get the list and let me know?"

"Please is the magic word Roy. It works wonders."

I realize I should have said please. I always try to be polite. I put it down to my running late.

"Of course, sorry, please Sue. I'd appreciate your help, and honestly, I need it."

Sue laughs. Her cheeky laugh I think.

"I honestly doubt that Roy. I think you do pretty well on your own, but it's nice to think I'm needed, even if it's just for a damn list."

It's my turn to laugh. She is a cheeky lady, and I'm pretty sure I've never met anyone else quite like her.

"I'll see what I can do this morning. Can I call you later?"

"Yes. Yes please. I should be home sometime between ten thirty and eleven, no later than eleven. But now I really must run."

"Okay, okay, I know you don't want to chat with me. Off you go. Shouldn't keep the family waiting."

Sue hangs up.

Funny really. Of course I could keep the family waiting. Well, really no-one would wait. Lisa would drop Michael off and leave, and he would be quite happy playing with his team mates. Still, I think a commitment is a commitment, and I promised I would be there.

145

I arrive at the soccer ground at eight thirty-five. The boys are on the pitch already, warming up. I think the game starts at nine but I can't remember being told that.

Lisa is leaning against her car, talking to a couple, other parents I suppose. I wander over and she introduces me to Alan Walker and Jane Henderson, parents of two of the boys playing in the same team as Michael.

Lisa looks at her watch for the second time since I arrived. "I'd better go." She says. "I left the other kids home. And you'll be alright to stay around and drive Michael home?" She adds.

"No problem Lisa. I promised I'd be here and here I am. What time do they kick off?"

"Nine." Alan Walker answers.

Lisa leaves and I'm left alone with Alan and Jane, and a few other parents in different areas along the side lines.

"If you'll excuse me. I am going to move over to those benches near the netball court fence. I'm not sure I want to stand up for another ninety minutes."

They both make noises indicating they understand.

I head into the club-room first and buy a cup of coffee, my second for the day, carry the coffee to one of the benches and sit down.

Damn! I was going to pick up a copy of the Globe on the way, so I could read it at the game. The call with Sue Weissman going longer than planned threw my schedule out a little.

I sit in the sun and wave to Michael when he's on my side of the pitch, so he knows I'm there.

The match starts right on nine.

Michael plays on the wing and he puts in a great cross, allowing his team to score the first goal. He also scores a goal himself, from quite a long way out and he's grinning from ear to ear as he runs back to his position for the next kick-off.

They break for half time and I walk on to the pitch and congratulate him on his goal. When the half time break finishes I walk back to the bench.

The second half is underway when I hear a car pull up on the road, somewhere behind me. I turn and see a small, blue Japanese model, with two girls in it. The girls get out of the car and walk on to the netball court. One is bouncing a ball.

The day is quite warm already and I'm surprised to see that both girls are wearing hooded jackets. Grey hoodies and blue jeans.

I alternate between watching Michael's team play and the girls practising throwing goals.

I suddenly realize how I really must be getting old.

Grey hoodies and blue jeans are the clothes that Skye and her friend were wearing when they were supposedly seen in the Lismore Square Shopping Centre.

Could this be them? I wonder.

That would explain the hoodies, wouldn't it?

But why would they be in such public places? Like the Shopping Centre and now here, out in the open? *It doesn't make sense to me.*

I get up and start to walk around the fence to the opening that leads to the netball courts. The girls see me moving and stop throwing the ball.

Then I hear, "Poppa Roy, Poppa Roy. Thank goodness I've found you."

It's Sue Weissman, walking towards me from the direction of the club-room, with a cup of coffee in one hand and some sheets of paper in the other.

When I turn around, the girls are heading towards the beat up old car. They get in and drive away and it's too far away for me to read the registration plate. I can see the *P* plate on the back quite clearly, but not the numbers and letters. My eyes aren't what they used to be.

I turn back to Sue.

She looks quite lovely this morning, in tight jeans and a small top, her blonde hair flowing as she walks.

"Good morning again, Sue. That was probably the most in-opportune timing. I'm glad to see you of course, but I think those girls, the two who were on the netball court were Skye Burrows and a friend."

"Wow!" Sue looks genuinely surprised. "Are you sure Roy?"

"I would say in the high nineties, if I had to put a percentage on my sureness. It was the grey hoodies and blue jeans that prompted me to get up and look closer. Although it took me longer than it should have to associate the clothing with them.

And, when I thought about it, wearing hoodies on such a nice warm morning should have seemed a bit unusual as well, but it took a while to sink in. But when I was walking towards them, Skye's hoodie slipped off a bit and I got a good look at her face. It was Skye, I'm sure."

"Shit! Oops, sorry. I'm so sorry Roy, honestly. I didn't even notice them. I was just glad to find you."

149

"No problems Sue. At least we can be one hundred percent sure now that she's still here in Lismore. She's alive and she seems okay. That, at least, substantiates my theories. Also she's probably staying somewhere not too far from here. Otherwise why come to this particular netball court?"

I'm relieved that my theories are proving to be correct. Using spirit writing is simple but there is no guarantee the results are accurate, or even reasonably so. This time, it seems, they are.

"Do you think we should call the police?" Sue asks. "And did you get much of a description of the car?"

I give it some consideration.

"No Sue, I wouldn't suggest we call the police. We really can't tell them much, can we?

And as for the car; I find a lot of the smaller cars look almost the same. But I think it's an early model, maybe twenty years old, Nissan, Toyota, Mitsubishi or maybe Mazda. It was too far away for me to see the badges. But I think it's probably something Japanese, and dark blue. I saw that it had *P* plates fitted but my old eyes couldn't make out the registration plate details I'm afraid."

"I'm not surprised. It was probably about fifty or sixty metres away and I'm not sure anyone could at that distance."

I walk back to the bench.

"Here Sue," I pat the bench beside me. "Sit down and show me what you've got for me."

"Here?" She looks around and smiles cheekily. "You really are an old devil, aren't you?"

I blush as she sits down close to me and unfolds the sheets of paper.

"Sorry. I couldn't resist." She says.

She hands me the sheets of paper. They have names, addresses and some telephone numbers on them.

"I actually had this list when we spoke earlier. Joanne dropped it in at the office the afternoon after we three met. I took it home and forgot about it when we were talking this morning. Guess you caught me half-asleep. Anyway, when I realized I had it, I got dressed and drove around until I found the right soccer field."

"Did you check out the two names I gave you?"

I know already that she wouldn't have been able to resist looking. She's an investigative journalist after all.

"Yes I did, as you probably thought I would. But I don't think the list will be much help."

I scan down the first page then the second. There is no Chris amongst the list of students.

"Wait a minute Sue. What about Janet Walsh here? Did you notice her? She's listed as a student teacher."

Sue leans over my shoulder. It feels good being close to her.

"Damn!" She says. "I honestly didn't look at the teachers. I was concentrating on the kids' names."

"If that was the student teacher with Skye, she would be young and probably still driving on *P* plates. We could have our Janet."

"Wow Poppa Roy! Sue exclaims, putting her arm around me. "Whatever you call your magic, it certainly seems to work."

"Yes it does. Lately anyway."

I hadn't noticed the soccer match was finished.

"Hi Poppa Roy," a young voice says. It's Michael.

I edge away from Sue a little and stand.

"Hi Michael. Good game. By my counting it was about three–one. Well done."

"Four–one actually." Michael replies. "You might have missed the last one. I think you were busy talking to the lady."

"Lady? Oh yes, sorry Sue."

152

I'm just a little flustered. Michael's right. I was busy with the lady. My mind was anyway.

"Michael, this is Sue Weissman, a journalist with the Globe newspaper. And Sue, this is Michael, my eldest grandson, Lisa's son."

"Hi Michael," Sue says, smiling and holding out her hand. "Nice to meet you."

"Good morning Miss Weissman," Michael answers politely, shaking her hand. "Mum said that you might be working with Poppa Roy on the case of the missing girl, Skye. Is that why you're here?"

"Very astute young man. I haven't decided what I'm doing yet, but Miss Weissman brought me some papers which might just help. We were just going over them."

I hold up the sheets of paper to show him I was telling the truth, although it's probably my guilty conscience which leads me to do it, rather than any expectation on Michael's part.

"Do you know Skye Burrows, Michael?" Sue asks. "Was she in the same school?"

It's an obvious question I guess, but I hadn't thought of asking it. When I did think about it, Michael would've probably passed Skye's house on the way to and from school.

"I know who Skye is." Michael replies. "I used to see her sometimes on the way to school. I didn't really know her but she seemed okay."

"And what about Janet Walsh, the student teacher?" Sue asks.

Michael nods, "Miss Walsh has been in a few classes of mine, just watching and learning I guess. The regular teachers took the classes. I can't remember her saying much. She seemed alright though, but she looks very young to be a teacher.

Is she involved in the Skye Burrows thing somehow?"

Sue is very quick. She seems to have had anticipated the question and had an answer ready. "No, she isn't." She says. "Just a name which was mentioned yesterday but I had no idea who she is until we looked at the list just now."

"Okay young man, if you're finished, I guess I'd better get you home." I say to Michael.

"Sue, is there any way you can check an address for that other person?" *I don't want Michael to know we're checking on Janet Walsh. I really have no idea if Sue has that ability, or contacts with someone who has.*

154

"I think I can." Sue replies. "Will you be home this afternoon Poppa Roy? I'm not sure if I can get the details today, but just in case."

"After I take this young champion home." I say, putting my arm around Michael's shoulders. "I'll head to my place. Allowing some time to talk to Lisa, I think I'd be there within about an hour or so."

"Great, I'll either see you this afternoon or call you if I can't find anything." She says.

She walks off, heading towards her car which is parked near the club-room.

I think I'd like it if she drops in this afternoon anyway. But maybe I shouldn't.

"She seems nice," says Michael.

"She is." I agree with him of course. "And very good at what she does."

"I've heard mum say some things about Miss Weissman that aren't nice." Michael says.

"She was talking on the telephone to someone but she stopped talking when she noticed I was in the room."

"Yes Michael, I'm afraid we're often quick to judge people when we don't really know them. It's a problem we humans have. I try to treat all people as being good until they give me some reason to think otherwise.

It's easier that way. You don't have to worry about whether you like them or not, or if they're good or bad, just accept at first.

Do you know what people mean when they say that some things are black or white, while others are grey?" I ask as I unlock the car and we get in.

"Yes," Michael answers. "I think so. Black or white means you make up your mind and have a definite opinion one way or the other. But being grey means you don't decide, you just accept, or something like that."

"Very good Michael. And that's about right.

I once made up a little adage, to enter a competition. It goes something like; *as I get older I find that most things are grey, and not just my hair.*"

"Does that mean you don't judge as much as you used to?" Michael asks. "Or that you don't care as much?"

"Probably bit of both actually. You learn that things that some people seem to care about passionately probably don't really matter. The world will keep turning the way it always has, and night will follow day."

156

"What about things like climate change?" Michael asks. "Surely that's something we should all care about."

"More grey I'm afraid. Whose truth do we accept? Some scientists say that climate change and global warming are a reality and they're caused by burning fossil fuels. While others insist it's just a cyclic thing and that the earth will get cooler again.

Then you read that the volcanoes which erupted in Iceland a few years ago put more carbon monoxide and carbon dioxide into the atmosphere than humans have for the last hundred and fifty years, or more. If that's true, what point is there in trying to burn less fossil fuels.

Another volcano could erupt tomorrow and we would be back where we started.

Another thing, only a few years ago there was a real panic in the papers and on television, about holes in the ozone layer and how civilisation would be affected, particularly in Australia.

Now you don't hear anyone talking about holes in the ozone layer."

Were they there? Were they real? Are they still up there somewhere? Do they matter?

"It's just gone quiet. Gone grey I guess."

We pulled up at Lisa's house while we were talking. I decide I should go in and spend an hour or so visiting, so I walk up to the front door with Michael.

Chapter Thirteen

My visit with Lisa is pleasant enough and she's delighted that Michael played well. She says they will make sure his father knows when he calls that evening, from Orange, or wherever he is.

Thankfully Michael doesn't mention Sue and the fact that she'd been at the match. I hoped that my talk about black or white and grey may have had some sort of positive effect.

Perhaps he just wants to be tactful, not to give his mother any more ammunition, and just to judge Sue as he found her. I hope so.

I leave her house after about forty five minutes, and drive home.

The case is on my mind, but so is Sue. I wonder what she's really like. Is she the slut that Lisa and her friends think she is, or is she just a reasonably pretty woman who uses her sexuality to get doors open, doors which may have otherwise been closed to her and the Globe.

And Sue did complain about Ken Wood trying to get on with her. *Would a slut complain?*

I'm undecided about if I want to find out.

I've been home about an hour when the telephone rings. It's Sue.

"Poppa Roy," Sue sounds excited. "Poppa Roy, I think we have another problem. Can I come over now? And I mean right now. I'm only a few minutes away, just down the street."

"Of course you can Sue. What's wrong?"

"I'm on my way. Please don't answer the telephone until I get there. Give me five."

With that, she hangs up.

What a strange call.

I'm wondering why I shouldn't answer the telephone when it rings.

A number I don't know appears on the screen. I write it down, and note the time.

Sue's car pulls up out front and I watch her hurry out of the car, slam the door and almost run towards my front door.

I think she's either desperate to see me or something is very, very, wrong. I unlock the door before she gets there and hold it open for her.

"Did she call?" Sue asks.

"There was a call Sue. I didn't answer it because you said I shouldn't, but I made a note of the number. What's going on and why couldn't I answer it?"

"Phew! Thank goodness I caught you,"

Not much of an explanation I think.

"Roy, I just had a call from someone who says she knows all about Skye Burrows.

Somehow she knows you may be involved and when I said you can probably help, she demanded I give her your telephone numbers."

"Do you have any idea who it was Sue?"

Sue shakes her head. "No I don't. But for some reason I think it might be someone who knows where Skye is, perhaps this Janet person? But really that's just a guess. And when I tried to ask her name, whoever it was just hung up."

I'm about to say something about not jumping to conclusions when the telephone rings again.

Sue puts her hand on mine to stop me picking up the receiver. "Do you have a speaker phone?"

I nod and she mouths some words, which I take to mean '*turn the speaker on.*' At the same time she takes out her own telephone and I assume she switches on some recording feature or other.

The telephone has rung three times by the time I pick it up.

"Hello. Sorry to keep you waiting."

I can hear someone breathing heavily.

Then a woman's voice says, "Mr Addams? Is that Mr Addams?"

"Yes. This is Roy Addams. What can I do for you?"

"Mister Addams," the voice says. "My name is Janet Walsh."

Then the voice is quiet.

"Hi Janet, I think I know who you are. How can I help?"

"What, what do you know?" Janet asks, sounding very nervous. Sue scowls at me. I assume she doesn't agree with me saying that. But I've found people will generally open up more if they believe you already know something.

"I understand you're a student teacher at the school Skye Burrows attended before she went missing. And, if I'm right, you and Skye are friends. And I believe I saw you with Skye, today at the netball courts."

Yes, I'm guessing a little but I decide my approach is better than just being quiet and hoping the other person says all you want to hear.

162

"Yes Mr Addams. Yes, you did see us at the netball courts, but how did you know it was me?"

"Let's just say it was my brilliant detective work, or just a lucky guess. Whatever suits you to believe. But, if I'm right, it doesn't really matter does it?"

"No. No, I guess not." Janet Walsh says. Then, "Mr Addams, I'm worried. Skye is missing."

I raise my eyebrows to Sue and she does the same to me, and shrugs her shoulders.

"I'm sorry Janet, but I know Skye has been missing from her home, for a few weeks now, but I thought that she was with you and that you were keeping her safe."

I'm guessing again.

"Skye has been with me." Janet says quietly. "But I'm not sure how you know that. Did her mother tell you?"

Now I'm truly surprised. I honestly have no idea what she is talking about.

"Her mother? No Janet. Listen, can we meet somewhere? Perhaps we'd better start at the beginning."

"Yes. Yes, that's a good idea Mr Addams." Janet says. "But can we meet soon? I'm really worried about Skye now."

Now I'm worried. A few hours ago I really had no idea where Skye was. Then, when I thought she was with Janet Walsh, I was relieved. I thought Skye was safe. But now? I don't know what to think. And how is Joanne Burrows involved?

"Where are you Janet? Perhaps I can come there. Or would it be easier for you to come here? I'm only a few minutes out of town."

"Can I come to your place please Mr Addams?" Janet asks. "I'm in a share apartment and, well, there is no privacy here. I don't want to go to the police and I don't know who else I can trust. Miss Weissman said you might be able to help."

"And I hope I can, but all I can promise is that I will try. Until I know what's going on anyway."

Maybe a little too straight to the point, I guess, but I have absolutely no idea what I'm up against.

"And Janet," I say this after Sue makes hand signals to me and points to herself. "Miss Weissman is here now. We're helping each other on this case on the understanding that nothing appears in her paper until the case is solved.

I prefer that she stays, but I'm sure she'll be happy to leave if you would rather she's not here."

Sue smiles when I say I'd prefer her to stay and blows me a kiss, but pouts when I suggest that she would be happy to leave. I know she wouldn't be, but I feel pretty well obliged to offer to be alone if it's what Janet wants.

"Miss Weissman?" Janet asks. "Oh the reporter I called? Yes it's fine if she's there, if she's helping."

Sue smiles again and squeezes my hand.

I give Janet directions to find my house and she hangs up, promising to be here within ten minutes.

"Thank you Roy," Sue says, coming closer. "I'm not sure I could have stood it if she said she wanted to be alone with you. I think the suspense would have killed me and I would've had to have been in another room with a secret microphone, or at least a glass or something like it up against the wall."

"We are working on this together, aren't we? So I didn't tell any lies."

The small blue car pulls up after only about five minutes, and a young woman gets out. She's still wearing her blue jeans but the hoodie has gone, exchanged for a light blue shirt.

I answer the door and let Janet in. To me, and I'm not really a very good judge of ages, she looks about twenty two or twenty three. I introduce myself and then Sue, realising as I did that I should have done the gentlemanly thing and introduced Sue first.

Too much to remember sometimes, I think, these manners.

We sit in the lounge.

I ask Janet if she would like something to drink and she asks for a glass of water. Sue offers to get it and she's soon back with it.

"Janet."

I'm not really sure how to get the discussion started.

"Perhaps it would be easier if you just explain what's going on and we'll ask questions to clarify things as we go along. Is that alright with you?"

Janet nods her agreement, but looks at Sue and says, "Mr Addams, you said that nothing will appear in the media until the case is all over. Does that include anything I say today? I mean, can I talk without being worried that it will be in Monday's paper?"

"Definitely!" Sue says before I can reply. "We have an agreement with Poppa Roy, sorry Mr Addams, that nothing will be released until the case is over. Then the Globe will have exclusive rights to the story. And my editor has signed off on the agreement."

I realise that Sue is really stretching the truth a little as the agreement only extends to my involvement, but it doesn't matter. She's giving her word and without Sue's involvement, the Globe won't have a story anyway.

Janet nods again and begins her explanation.

"Skye wasn't happy at home because, well because she found out that her mother, Joanne, was having an affair. Skye left school early one day because she didn't feel well but when she got home she found her mother with another man. Skye saw them in the bedroom but she wasn't sure if her mother saw her."

"Do you know who the man is?" I interrupt.

"Yes, sort of anyway," Janet answers. "It's a man named Chris something or other.

Apparently he works for the same organisation as Paul Burrows so he knows when Mr Burrows is busy elsewhere. Or something like that."

She continues.

"When Skye saw them she was upset and ran out of the house. She headed back to school and that's where she met me. We had spoken a few times prior to this incident, so she sort of knew me.

I wasn't sure what to do. Skye didn't want me to tell any of the counsellors, so I offered to let her stay with me, at my place for a while. She went home that night and didn't say anything but the next morning she came straight to my place. So I took the day off to be with her."

"You asked if Joanne told us something," Sue interrupts. "Did Joanne know Skye was with you?"

"Yes she did." Janet answers. "Not at first, but I think Skye got sick of me insisting she should let her mother know she was okay, so she called her, about four or five days ago. That's why we started going out. We were careful about covering up a little but we thought that Joanne would've told the police that Skye was safe and people would stop looking for her.

"But she hasn't." Sue says. "She hasn't said a thing, and we saw her as late as yesterday."

I was quiet, listening and absorbing. It seems to me that Joanne probably didn't say anything because she couldn't admit she knew why Skye left home, not to Paul or to anyone else. It would probably have meant she would have had to confess to having an affair with this Chris guy.

168

But this is just conjecture on my part.

"Go on Janet, why are you worried about Skye now?" Sue prompts.

"When we saw you this morning, we had no idea who you were." Janet indicates that she means me. "Then we heard the words *Poppa Roy*. I think Miss Weissman was shouting out to you. Anyway we went home straight away, and sat talking. Skye told me that Joanne had said someone named Poppa Roy might come looking for her, but she wasn't sure. Anyway, when we heard your name this morning, we thought you had found us, or found Skye.

Skye decided she needed to either go home, or go somewhere else, somewhere further away, so she called Joanne again.

I'm not a hundred percent sure what happened next. Joanne must have told Skye she, or someone anyway, would collect her. So Skye packed up the few things she had with her and waited.

After about half an hour a car pulled up.

Skye saw that Joanne was driving so she went out to the car and began to get in. I went out to wave her goodbye. As she started to slide into the car an arm appeared from the back seat, and grabbed her, and the car began moving. Skye was half out of the car, she had one leg out as the car went faster towards the corner.

She screamed as her leg disappeared inside and the door closed. I could see three people in the car through the back window. Skye and her mother in the front and a man in the back.

"Do you know who the man was Janet?"

Janet shakes her head, "No I don't. I had assumed it might have been this Chris man, but I don't know."

"And the car?" Sue asked. "Did you get a good look at it?"

She shakes her head again. "I know it wasn't Joanne's car. Skye said so when it pulled up, but we could see her mother was driving it. I do know it was a Ford because I recognised the blue oval insignia, but I don't know what model nor how old it was. Oh, and it was green, dark green, if that helps. But I didn't think of looking at the registration plates until it was almost around the corner. I'm sorry."

The younger woman is sobbing quietly and Sue puts her arms around her.

I leave them alone to look for my writing pad and a pen. *This has been a lot for my tired old head to absorb and I*

170

need to make some notes while I can still remember the details.

So this Chris works at the same place as Paul Burrows. Do we know where Paul Burrows works? I guess the police must know, so I write a message to myself with *CHECK POLICE?* Next to it.

It appears that Joanne must have known that Skye was safe for up to five days, but she said nothing. Again I think of all possible reasons. The most likely reason, I decide is that she didn't want her affair with Chris to be made public.

But what would Joanne have done if the police found Skye?

Skye had basically forced Joanne's hand by calling home.

I decide the affair probably would have had to come out in the end anyway and that, at best, Joanne must have been hoping to buy time.

But why? For what? What was likely to change?

Perhaps hoping Skye might accept the situation, or it would blow over somehow.

Perhaps Joanne and this Chris man had been planning to pick up Skye all along.

But why? To do what?

171

They might have planned to silence her somehow.

But would a mother do that to her own daughter?

I decide that I am perhaps reading too much into it and that Joanne may have only intended to take Skye away somewhere so she could talk to her and convince her to keep quiet about everything.

But would Skye keep quiet? And what if she refused? What would the next step be?

In any event, I conclude, Skye is now in real trouble.

I re-join the ladies.

They're still together, talking quietly. Sue smiles at me over Janet's shoulder.

"Where do we go from here ladies? Do we go straight to the police?"

"I'm not sure that's a good idea Roy." Suggests Sue. "Not yet anyway. Janet and I have been talking and she's worried about all the things she could be charged with.

Remember, Skye's a minor and Janet is an adult. The police could have a field day and we only have Janet's word that Skye was with her willingly.

And you know what the media might do with a potential teacher-student scandal, even if the Globe agrees not to print anything about it. If it came out somehow, the

172

general press would have a field day and make the most of it, whether there was anything sexual involved or not. It's cannon fodder for them, and either way, it'd be the end of Janet's career. And of course, we don't know what Joanne might say, regardless of any agreement."

I am almost afraid to ask but I have no choice. "I assume you ladies have a plan?"

Before they get a chance to answer, the telephone rings. It's Lisa.

"Hi dad. Thanks again for taking Michael this morning. Are you busy?"

I tell her I'm not.

"Listen, I have been baking today and I've just taken a batch of homemade scones and biscuits out of the oven. You know, the shortbread ones you like.

Anyway, I thought I would run some over but I just needed to make sure you're home. I didn't want to leave them on the front step where the ants will get them before you do."

Bless Lisa.

I thank her and end the call.

"Ladies, we have a small problem. My daughter is on the way over right now. We can either move the cars and you

173

two hide somewhere, or make up some story very quickly to explain who you are Janet, and why you're both here."

Sue looks out the window and shrugs her shoulders. "We probably won't have time to hide the cars, and it would be worse if we are seen driving away.

Leave Lisa to me. I'll come up with a story. I always do. You should read them in the paper one day.

Janet, just be ready to say you think you saw Skye in the Shopping Centre yesterday. Then make up whatever you like."

Janet looks confused but she nods.

Before we have the chance to say much more Lisa's car pulls up in front of the house.

She unlocks her car and gets out then reaches into the car for two small trays, biscuits and scones as promised.

Lisa looks at the two other cars in front of the house and shakes her head, then walks to the front door.

I have the door open already.

"Dad, what's going on? And whose cars are these?

"Hi Lisa, come in."

Lisa walks into the living room. Sue stands up, smiles and holds her hand out to Lisa.

"Hello again Lisa. That's twice in one day we've seen each other. And this is Jane Waters." Sue points to Janet.

"Blame me, Lisa." Sue says smiling. "Jane knows Skye Burrows and she thinks she saw Skye in the Square Shopping Centre yesterday as well. She rang me and I convinced her to come here and speak with Poppa Roy. I thought he might use some of his mumbo jumbo or whatever it is, and find out what's going on."

"But I thought you weren't going to get involved dad," Lisa says. "This certainly looks like you are."

"Not really." It's my turn to be a little creative. "When Sue spoke to me and told me that Jane was reluctant to go to the police because she's known to them, and not in a good way, I agreed she should come here. I thought if she tells me all she knows I might be able to use it and, well you sort of know what I do. Perhaps I can come up with some clues that I can let the police know about. They already have some idea that I pull clues and hints from somewhere and with me, they don't really have to know where from."

"So you will be involved won't you?" Lisa says, rather defiantly.

"I won't be involved in any investigation that they, or anyone else, know about. I've already given some ideas to

175

Ken Wood, and made some suggestions. I will let Sue know what I think and she'll present it as just being more ideas, clues, hopefully with some logic to back them up. Without me being mentioned if possible. But if she has to, she will simply say it was something I said in passing and she'll repeat that I'm not involved and don't want to be seen to be involved. But we've only just started talking here, so I don't have anything yet."

"Oh dad. I know mum didn't like whatever it is you do. She thought it is dangerous, some type of black magic. Now I'm more worried."

"Lisa, there is nothing to worry about I assure you. I just ask questions and the answers come from somewhere. I don't know where. You can think of it as praying if that makes it easier to accept. The trouble is your mother closed her mind to whatever good it might do because she couldn't understand it, and never really tried. I offered to show her quite a few times so she could see there was no danger involved and that it was simply writing, but she always refused.

Anyway, if I can do something simple to help the police find Skye Burrows, without really getting involved, I feel I have to. I can't just refuse to even try."

Lisa looked at me, then Sue and finally Janet, who still had tears in her eyes and looked like a scared waif, sitting alone on the lounge.

"I can see you've made up your mind dad, and that there's no point me saying any more.

Please, please be careful and Miss Weissman, I'm not sure how you will convince the police that dad isn't involved, but I'd appreciate if you could do your best."

"It will be best to simply say I was throwing about a few opinions and theories, following up on yesterday's conversation, and then highlight a few points that she thinks they should follow up on, her suggestions not mine."

"That sounds better I suppose dad, and thank you Miss Weissman. Dad, enjoy the scones and the biscuits. You should have told me you had guests and I would have brought some more."

Lisa is smiling but I know she's not happy and she's just putting on a brave face. "And good luck Miss Waters." She says to Janet, "I hope my dad can help, I honestly do"

I show Lisa to the door and she gives me a hug and a smile. "I mean it dad. Please be careful."

I hug her back and she walks to her car.

"Phew!" Says Sue. "Do you think she will buy that?"

"I'm not really sure what's going on here I'm afraid." Janet says. "But whatever was said made sense to me, except the mumbo jumbo bit."

"All in good time Janet. I'll explain later.

But first, before we were interrupted I asked if you ladies have a plan."

"We do and we don't Roy," Sue says. "We thought we should be able to find out where Paul works fairly easily. This isn't a big town and I could even ask Joanne, on the pretext that you want to talk to him. And you've already indicated that you do.

The main thing is, that Joanne can't know we're aware she's involved. Janet will need to try to proceed as if nothing has happened and we, you and I, must appear to be operating exactly as we said we would.

Finding Skye, and getting her away from whoever it is that's got her now, must be a priority of course. But if we don't do anything out of the ordinary, we stand a chance they won't panic and do something silly.

I think getting the police involved could be precipitous and, apart from putting a lot of pressure on Janet, it could also cause Joanne, and whoever has Skye, to panic. And that's the last thing we need."

I think about Sue's suggestions. I agree that making the situation public could have a disastrous effect on Janet, and her career, but I can't help thinking also that, as Skye is possibly now in very real danger, we need to act quickly. And, that we probably can't afford to let things develop over a long period. I think that might jeopardise Skye in some way. Which way to go?

We agree on a course of action.

Sue will call Joanne as soon as Janet leaves, and ask if it is possible for me to see Paul. If not today or tomorrow, then perhaps at work on Monday. We hope in this way, Joanne might be encouraged to say where he works.

I agree it's worth a try.

Sue says that after Janet leaves, she wants me to try to get more answers, based on our latest information, and that she wants to see what happens.

I'm a bit dubious. I've never tried it with another person in the room. When I express my doubts, Sue offers to leave if it doesn't seem to be working.

We agree that when Janet gets home, she will try to act as if nothing out of the ordinary has happened, and tell her flat-mates that Skye has gone back with her mother. Also, that it's unlikely there will be any immediate announcement in the

179

papers, as Skye's mother has agreed to keep everything low-key for Janet's sake.

And for her own sake in reality of course, as Joanne had known where Skye was, for the last week or so anyway.

That bit sounds plausible at least, and the three of us think it will work as long as Janet can keep up the pretence that nothing is wrong.

Janet hugs Sue, shakes my hand and leaves. She's leaving the two of us alone.

Chapter Fourteen

"Now how do we go about this, Poppa Roy?" Sue's intrigued that she might finally get to see some spirit writing as it happens.

I explain the basics and the importance of getting the questions down, as unambiguous as possible. Then the meditation bit and hopefully, interpretation of the results.

We sit at my desk with the pad of blank writing paper in front of us.

The questions we agree on are;

Is Skye Burrows alive? I decide this is still the most fundamental issue.

Is Skye Burrows in danger? Danger is relative, I realise, but I reason that the urgency to find and save her has to be related to the danger she is in. And I trust the spirits understand it that way too.

Is Skye Burrows still in Lismore?

Is Skye Burrows in a house?

Is Skye Burrows being kept a prisoner?

Does her mother know where she is?

Does Paul Burrows know where she is?

Does Skye Burrows want to go home?

Is the man Chris holding her prisoner?

Is the man Chris also Barry Fletcher?

Can you tell us Chris's other name?

What is his second name? His surname?

Is Skye Burrows safe?

Can we find Skye Burrows?

Will we find Skye Burrows?

Can we trust Janet Walsh?

All of the questions are on one single page and I tape it to the desk, in front of my computer screen.

"Now what do you want me to do?" Sue asks, sitting next to me.

"Well, honestly, I've got no idea if this will work. I've never tried going into my trance and meditating with someone else in the room. And, I don't know what will happen.

You being a sexy and pretty lady might not help. As far as me focussing I mean. As for the spirits, I don't know what impact you might have on them.

I'm willing to try, for Skye's sake. But it might help if you're not quite so close, maybe out of my line of sight when I look at the screen."

"Well!" Sue's mock indignation is cute. "A girl knows when she's not wanted.

Although you did say I'm sexy and pretty. I was beginning to wonder if you noticed. Thought I might be losing my touch."

Sue stands, kisses me on the cheek and moves her chair so it's almost behind me, sort of on a sixty degree angle, so she can still see the screen.

"And," I add as an after-thought. "I don't know what effect it might have on you if you concentrate on the screen for too long. So if you want to just observe, it may be better if you look away from time to time."

Sue reaches out and squeezes my arm. "I understand. I'll see you when you come back to me."

I bring up my favourite mantra, and try to decide what I'm going to analyse this time. I'm conscious that Sue's in the room and even though I can't see her, I know she's there.

Still, I reason, I've managed to access my spirits or whatever they are in daylight, twice, when I had no idea if I could, so this is worth a try.

The mantra is still, un-moving. *What will happen if I cause it to rotate? How will the colours blend? And, if it*

183

spins, how fast will it have to turn until all the colours blend to one? Will it be white, or some other colour? Is there a dominant colour? In my mind it spins, faster and faster.

o0o

"Poppa Roy," a soft voice beside me says. "Poppa Roy, are you okay?"

I'm awake and coherent, my eyes are open and someone, yes, Sue Weissman, is talking to me.

"Oh Poppa Roy. I was worried about you and if you would ever come back. Is this what you go through each time?"

"I honestly have no idea what I go through, or if it's the same each time. I just disappear from my usual consciousness, then emerge some time later. How long was I away?"

Sue looks at her watch. "Almost two hours. But when you went it was if you had died. You just seemed to fade away and, well, I was worried. I had no idea what to expect or if you'd come out of it."

Sue moves her chair alongside mine and has one arm around me. It's obvious she's worried.

"You can tell me what actually happened some other time," I suggested. "Do we have any writing?"

I switch on my desk light and Sue and I move forward. There is writing on the sheet, hopefully answers to our questions.

As is always the case, there are words in different areas of the sheet, some close enough to the questions to suggest they are responses plus others perhaps which, by their locations, don't appear to refer to any specific question.

Is Skye Burrows alive?

YES

I'm relieved to see this response.

Is Skye Burrows in danger?

??YES??

I assume the question marks are confirmation that the question is a little ambiguous. Danger is relative.

Is Skye Burrows still in Lismore?

YES NO YES

This suggests to me that Skye is in Lismore or somewhere close enough to Lismore to be regarded as part of the city, *perhaps a suburb,* I think. And yes, I remember that Lismore does have suburbs, although they are often not referred to.

Is Skye Burrows in a house?

????NO

Is Skye Burrows being kept a prisoner?

YES!!

Does her mother know where she is?

YES!!

Does Paul Burrows know where she is?

??NO

Does Skye Burrows want to go home?

???????

Is the man Chris holding her prisoner?

?????

Is the man Chris also Barry Fletcher?

??YES

Can you tell us Chris's other name?

?????

What is his second name? His surname?

TOPHR???

Is Skye Burrows safe?

NO

Can we find Skye Burrows?

YES

Will we find Skye Burrows?

????

Can we trust Janet Walsh?

??YES!!YES

Sue looks at the sheet of paper and shakes her head. "If I didn't see it with my own eyes I wouldn't believe it possible.

I mean, where does it come from?"

"I honestly have no idea. I don't know if it's from somewhere inside me, from something else, such as a spirit, or maybe from you. I just don't know but it seems to work. Well, usually anyway. Let's look at the rest."

I cut the sheet of paper from the desk top and rotate it ninety degrees, then another ninety and so on, examining all of the apparently random words, trying to find some logical phrases or other word combination.

As I start to turn the sheet for a fifth time when Sue almost shouts, "There. That looks like *S-t-r-e-b-e* doesn't it? Could that mean something?" She's pointing at some letters scrawled along the bottom of the page.

I agree, it does look like the word *Strebe* , but it's so far from any of the questions, and any other legible words, I can't make any plausible connection. And what does *Strebe* mean anyway?

"Roy," Sue says slowly. "Just a thought but have you considered that some words may be written backwards?"

I hadn't and I tell her so.

"*Strebe* could be *Eberts*," Sue says. "I know there are a few *Eberts* in Lismore. In fact we have one working at the Globe. He's only young, about eighteen or nineteen, a general office roustabout with some title or other. Could it mean *Eberts*?"

I look at the writing, then at Sue. That some words could be written backwards had never occurred to me before, yet it's so simple, and really fairly obvious. *I don't know how I overlooked the possibility. I should have at least considered it.*

Sue and I run over the sheet again. We study it from four orientations, but finally agree we can't see any other legible words, forwards of backwards. A lot of the writing is in italics and it's almost impossible to even make out letters, let alone words.

I summarise what the sheet is telling us; "Skye is alive but she is being held captive and she is in some sort of danger. Skye's mother knows where she is but Paul doesn't and the man Chris is Barry Fletcher and he may be the man that's holding Skye, in or near Lismore but not in a house.

And I think the **TOPHR** just means the man's name is Christopher, no more than that. But now we also have the name *Strebe* or *Eberts*. Where does that fit?"

"I wish I knew, Poppa Roy. I wish I knew." Chris says, shaking her head. She looks at her watch. It's almost five o'clock and the shadows are lengthening outside.

"Do you have any food in the house Roy?"

"Yes, I guess I do. I usually have a little bit of everything. But I normally only buy for one person. What do you have in mind?

"Why don't you show me where I might find things and you go and get some nice wine while I make dinner for us?"

Again I realise I had never thought of Sue in a domestic situation. And I like the thought, of her playing that role, and of us spending more time together.

"Well mister? What about it?" Sue asks, disturbing my thoughts.

"You don't have to do that Sue. We could go out somewhere."

"And risk running into Lisa again, or someone else from her coffee set? No, I think my idea is better, and it will be nice to be alone with you. But, if you don't want to,,"

189

"Of course I want to Sue."

I decide there's nothing I would like better at the moment.

"What do you prefer, red or white?"

Sue says she prefers red, merlot or something similar. I don't mind any similar red.

I show her where things are in the kitchen and my meagre pantry, leave her to cook whatever she can manage with the ingredients I have, and head to the bottle shop.

The shop is busy, it is Saturday night after all, and I'm away for about forty minutes.

When I arrive home, the house smells delightful; something is simmering on the stove. Sue tells me she has made up a pasta sauce, remembering I ordered pasta when we lunched together.

"By the way." She says. "You really need to check the use-by dates on some of the things you have in your pantry, especially the spices. I realise some of them are only recommended best-before dates but I think something like garlic salt which is three or four years out of date, could be a concern. You could kill yourself."

"Maybe, but I haven't. So I guess things which matter must be okay."

Sue smiles and shakes her head.

Actually there are a lot of things I haven't used or even looked at since Marie died. It wouldn't surprise me if most things were out of date.

I open a bottle of red to let the wine breathe, then set the table in the dining room. I can't quite remember which glasses are meant to be used for red wine so I put two near each setting. I can watch which one Sue uses and the other one can be for water. Finding a clean jug, I go into the kitchen and take a bottle of iced water from the refrigerator.

Sue has found an apron from somewhere. I didn't even know I had any, and she smiles at me over her shoulder as she stirs the pasta sauce. "Ready in about five." Sue says. "Do we have any parmesan cheese?"

I bend and open the freezer section of the refrigerator. I think there is a packet in there somewhere. That too has probably reached the manufacturer's use-by date but because it is frozen I don't think the use-by date actually counts. I find it, it's a new packet, which has never been opened.

I take a small bowl from the cupboard, cut the top of the cheese packet and pour some into the bowl then take the bowl and a spoon and put them in the centre of the dining room table.

Cheese, utensils, water and glasses. What have I forgotten? I remember, some people like salt and pepper on their pasta. I find a fancy set in the side-board and put them on the table with the cheese.

Candles! Should we have candles?

I think that may be over-doing it, so I decide against it.

"Would you prefer a bowl or a plate?" Comes from the kitchen. "I'd prefer a bowl if you can tell me where I might find one."

I go into the kitchen. Sue has the pasta noodles and sauce ready on the bench top, with tongs for the pasta and a ladle for the sauce. I smile and take two medium size bowls from the lower shelf in the pantry, rinse and dry them then place them on the bench top.

"Smells great Suzie. Thank you."

"Mmm, thanks. But perhaps you should try it first."

I let Sue take her pasta and sauce first, then I put some noodles in my bowl and spoon in some sauce.

"That doesn't look like nearly enough Roy." Sue remarks. "You make me look like a guts because I took more."

I smile. "It's enough for me, I assure you. Besides there's a tub of ice cream in the freezer and I'm saving space for that. It's only a week old by the way, nowhere near its use-by date."

Sue laughs and we take our meals into the dining room.

She picks up the wine bottle. "Shall I pour?"

"Please."

Suzie pours some of the wine into one of her glasses then hands it to me. I exchange it for my empty glass.

We clink glasses. "Friends." I say. I think it is a simple enough salute, which can really say everything, or nothing.

"Friends." Sue says, then sips her wine.

We eat our food quietly and sip the wine occasionally. Sue refills her glass when I'm only half way through mine.

"This is very pleasant Roy." Sue has almost finished her pasta and is starting on her third glass of wine. "But this wine is way too nice. I love it."

I smile. It should be nice; it was the most expensive Merlot I could find in the bottle shop. I figured we, and the night, were worth it.

When we finish our pasta I pick up the bowls and take them into the kitchen. "Now, would mademoiselle care for some ice cream? Only vanilla I'm afraid. It's my favourite."

"Mine too, would you believe?" Sue says. "Plain vanilla with no topping, no nuts, nothing to spoil it."

"Bingo, just how I like it. Two ice creams coming up."

I take out two clean bowls and put two scoops of ice cream in each.

Did Sue know somehow that I also only like plain ice cream, I wonder, or is it a lucky coincidence that we both like the same thing?

When I go back into the dining room, Sue is smiling with that semi-glazed look people get when they have had just a little too much to drink. The bottle is empty. I had two glasses so I guess she probably had four.

I put the ice cream and a spoon in front of her and she starts eating it immediately, as if she is starving.

"Wow! This is great ice cream." Sue says. "Really smooth and creamy."

I nod and smile and eat mine slowly, watching Sue. Her eyes are drooping already. I realize it's been a long day, for her as well. And neither of us had time to eat anything earlier.

When I finish my ice cream, Sue tries to stand, saying something about doing the dishes before we relax. Her effort

194

to stand doesn't get too far and she holds on to the table with one hand and the side-board with the other. "Poppa Roy Addams! What have you done to me? I can normally drink much more than four glasses."

I move quickly to her side and put one arm around her waist to help her stand.

"Perhaps you had better lie down for a while Sue. Too much wine too quickly on an empty stomach I think."

"You just want me in your bed, don't you Poppa Roy?" Sue says smiling, and reaching for me.

"I need you fit and healthy in the morning Sue. We have a young lady to find, remember? Come on. The bed in the spare room is made up and ready."

I hold her up. She doesn't exactly stagger but she is reeling a little and seems unable to walk in a straight line. I lead her into the spare bedroom and hold her with one arm as I turn back the bed clothes.

I hold her arm and Sue collapses on to the bed. "I think I just need to lie down for a while. Then I'll be fine."

I pull the covers over her and sit on the edge of the bed. "Goodnight sweet Sue. See you in the morning."

I kiss her softly on the cheek and switch off the light as she lays there smiling, already half asleep.

Back in the dining room I take the dishes and glasses into the kitchen.

Thankfully I have a dish-washer and I rinse the pots and plates and stack the dish-washer shelves then turn it on before I head towards my bed-room. It has been a long day.

I look in on Sue. She is sleeping peacefully, her long hair spread on the white pillow. She is a special lady and I have grown to like her, a lot.

I think about what might, perhaps, be, and sigh. If only.

o0o

It's seven am and I'm awake.

I put on a light dressing gown and check on Sue in the other bedroom. I think she's asleep but as I turn to leave I hear, "I like my coffee white, with one sugar please. And can you tell me where the bathroom is please?

She is obviously awake.

"Good morning Sue. The bathroom is straight opposite, and I'll be back in a few minutes with some coffee."

When I come back with the coffee, Sue isn't there. She comes in looking radiant, in one of my shirts. It's

196

obviously too large for her and she's wearing it as a dress, with nothing underneath, or so it seems.

She kisses me on the cheek, slips back into the bed and pats the bed beside her. "I hope you are going to join me."

The coffee mugs are on the bed-side table and I sit carefully on the bed and lean back against the bed-head. She snuggles next to me and she does look lovely. "Sorry about last night Roy, honestly. How many glasses of wine did I have anyway?"

"Four I think Sue, or maybe a bit more. I wasn't really counting. But that was a lot on an empty stomach. How do you feel this morning? Ready to face the day?"

"Roy, I honestly wish we didn't have to. I'd rather just stay here. But we do don't we? We need to find Skye."

"We do." I agreed. I put my arm around her shoulders and held her. "And thank you for saying you'd rather stay here. It means a lot."

Sue sat up a little. "Come here and kiss me you silly man. There's nowhere else I'd rather be right now. And if you can't work that out you're not as good a detective as I thought you were."

A telephone rings somewhere.

197

Sue breaks from my arms. "Shit! That's mine. Can you get my handbag for me please Roy?"

I remember I unplugged my telephone last night and hadn't plugged it back in, so I do that at the same time and take the remote handset with me.

Sue's phone is still ringing. The caller is obviously patient and the call must be urgent.

She fishes the telephone from her bag and answers it. Sue raises her eyebrows to me and I gather it's something to do with the case.

I listen, but I could only hear one side of the conversation.

"Oh hi Joanne. Sorry it took me a while to find my phone. I'm not home and I was scrambling in my bag to find it.

And how are you?

No, no developments this end. I've spoken with Poppa Roy quite recently." She smiles when she says this and reaches for my hand. "But although he maintains that Skye is alive and still in Lismore he's no closer to finding out exactly where she is.

The police? No, he isn't talking to the police. Well he did have one meeting but all that was really said was that he's not involved, as we agreed.

Yes, Mr Addams would still like to talk to Paul.

When? I think he said possibly tomorrow or Monday. Does Paul work locally? Mr Addams would like to talk with him during the day on Monday if that's possible. No, I really don't know what about.

Now?

Yes I could come over now. Is there a problem?

Okay Joanne. I can be there in about forty minutes if that's alright. Right, see you then."

Sue finishes the call

"Wow! The plot thickens. But we now know a little more. Paul works for the local Department of Housing. He's an inspector and he's often out on the road, doing inspections. Joanne isn't sure if Paul will be in the office on Monday but she said she'll check and let me know.

And she said she needs to see me as soon as possible. She says it's something to do with the article I wrote about Skye being seen in the Shopping Centre. And I said I'll meet her at her place. What do you think Roy?"

My mind is in a bit of a spin. Apart from the fact that I don't want her to leave, I'm worried.

This is something neither of us expected. I wonder what it's all about.

"It could be a trap Sue. I don't know how or what but, oh, I don't know why, but it sounds fishy. Maybe you shouldn't go."

"But why should I let you have all the action?" Sue says, feigning a pout of sorts. "And I think I'm old enough and big enough to take care of myself. Besides it's daytime. I can't imagine anything would happen during the day."

Sue comes closer, takes my arm and pulls it around her again. "I was really looking forward to spending some quiet time with you Roy, talking about your mumbo jumbo stuff and finding out what makes you tick. It looks like I will have to wait I'm afraid.

But Joanne is usually short and sharp, and she always seems to be in a hurry. I could be back within an hour."

She turns her face to me and we kiss. An interesting kiss. To me it seems like both of us are testing, tasting but tentatively testing, not sure. At least that's how it feels to me.

"I'll be back," Sue says, breaking away. "Can I borrow this shirt? I'll race home and get changed then go to her place. And you don't go anywhere please, and keep your telephones on in case I need you."

She gets out of the bed and slips her skirt on, gathers up her other things and is out of the door.

200

Chapter Fifteen

I watch through the window as Sue walks quickly to her car, my shirt billowing about her. She waves as she gets in, closes the door and starts the engine.

She is an attractive lady, I decide, and I like her a lot. As a person and as a woman.

I honestly had no intention of getting involved with another woman, and, even though I have sort of known Sue for a year or two, I'd never thought of her that way.

But now? What's different?

She just seems much more human to me. Much more of a desirable woman than I'd ever thought possible. But I'm an old man, I remind myself. Is she genuinely interested in me? All the messages tell me she is, if I'm reading them correctly.

Looking at my telephone for the first time this morning, I see I had two calls last night. One from an unlisted number and the other from Lisa. The one from Lisa came through about eleven pm. Very late for her to be calling. I wonder what's wrong.

I decide to call her before I do anything else.

Lisa answers on the second ring.

"Dad! Dad are you alright?"

Lisa sounds as if she is in a panic about something. I assure her that I'm fine and ask her what the problem is.

"I was picking up Michael last night and I passed your place about ten thirty. And that Sue Weissman's car was still there, so I thought something might have been wrong."

I don't think for a moment that she imagined there was something wrong. I think she is fishing.

"Yes Lisa. Sue's car was here all night actually. But it's gone now.

"What do you mean all night?"

"Exactly that Lisa. We had dinner but Sue had four glasses of wine and I insisted she shouldn't drive. She slept in the spare bedroom."

"Oh dad. What's going on between you and her? I'm worried about you."

"Lisa, I promise you, Sue slept in the spare bed. I haven't made the bed so you can come and check if you like. And nothing is going on, but if I wanted it to, I think I'm old enough to make up my own mind."

"Oh, of course you are dad, but I worry about you and I don't want you hurt. You know how I feel."

"I know how you feel Lisa, and thank you. And I'm okay but I must go now, sorry."

I hang up the phone. She said how she feels and I've told the truth and I decide there's no more to add. Talking to her won't change how she feels and anyway, I have things I want to do.

Back in my study, I sort out the pages from my various writing sessions, putting the ones concerning Skye Burrows into chronological order.

Sue picked up on the fact that some of the writing appears backwards on the most recent page. Maybe some of the earlier, seemingly unintelligible words are backwards as well.

I find a series of letters on one of my earlier pages. **S-T-E-R-O-F**. And there's another **H-S-L-A-W**.

There is no doubt in my mind now that *hslaw* means *Walsh*, and it should have led me to *Janet Walsh* sooner. But as it appears along the top edge of a page, I had no reason to link it with any other words on that sheet.

Sterof I assume, might mean *forest*, but to an actual *forest* or a surname? It's on the page with my first questions about Barry Fletcher. *Is Fletcher's surname actually Forest?*

This business can get so confusing, I tell myself.

204

I look at the clock and see that Sue has been gone for forty minutes. She should be there by now. But even if they don't chat too much, I decide it's unlikely I'll see her for another hour or perhaps a little longer.   With a fresh cup of coffee in front of me, I read the news on my favourite web site. The international news is much the same as any other day. The United States is engaged in a minor war somewhere or other and the Secretary of State has issued a statement condemning a few countries which are not aligned as he feels they should be, and others which are involved but are not playing on the US team.

Nothing new I decide.

The national Australian news is a bit more interesting. There's a trial starting in another state, concerning the alleged abduction and murder of a young girl thirty years before. I know a little about the case and wonder how the police have managed to gather enough evidence to arrest and prosecute someone after all this time, when surely any material evidence would be long gone.

I read some of the detail and see that a lot of the prosecution case seems to be based on hearsay. Always a difficult thing to prove, particular if relying on thirty year old memories.

Then there's an article on Australia's Prime Minister, the fifth one in six years. My opinion is much like that expressed by a lot of people. That perhaps the number of changes come about because politicians these days seem to be interested in short term personal gain, rather than long term policies. The last guy was too much of a totalitarian anyway and something had to happen. *At least that seemed to be the common opinion.* At the time, I remember several people describing it as a '*democratically elected dictatorship.*'

My telephone rings, dragging my attention away from the internet.

I find the handset and answer it.

"Mr Addams," the voice says. "You didn't listen to me before and I know you are involved in the case of Skye Burrows, who is still missing."

I say nothing. It's the man who called himself Barry Fletcher last time he called.

"Mr Addams, now Miss Sue Weissman is also missing. I know you're waiting for a call from her but it won't happen. The two of you have been meddling and trying to find Skye, even though I spoke with both of you, and to your daughter. You just don't seem to realise how serious I am.

If you go to the police, or interfere further, in any way, forget seeing Miss Weissman again, and Skye Burrows might just disappear for good."

The man hangs up.

I sit and look at my cup of coffee, just sitting there. It's going cold and Sue is missing, but everything else in the world is acting as it should.

Nothing in the overall universe has changed.

But, I think, my whole world has just changed. Maybe not turned upside down but certainly turned on its side.

It seems obvious to me that Joanne Burrows must be behind this and she somehow enticed Sue to her house, only to be grabbed by someone, perhaps this Chris, maybe Chris Eberts or Chris Forest. The same thing that happened to Skye Burrows yesterday.

I haven't felt so devastated since my wife died.

My seeking Skye has possibly led to her being in much more danger, and now it appears Sue Weissman, the lively, cheeky and friendly Sue Weissman, who I'm just beginning to appreciate, is also in danger.

Devastated and totally deflated.

Getting my thoughts into some sort of logical order seems impossible.

207

I have a head full of what could be clues, but I have no idea what to do with them.

And Sue keeps popping up in my thoughts. Sue Weissman, a lady I don't really know, but one who seems to want to know me better, and I had been starting to feel the same way.

Yes I had! I tell myself.
And I don't need much convincing.

I sit at my desk with a clean white sheet of paper in front of me, and turn on the desk lamp.

Now what information do I really have?

I draw a circle in the middle of the page. I write Joanne Burrows' name in the circle. To me, it seems like everything centres on her.

I draw arrows out from the circle. Really there are four but one is tentative at best. The four are Jan De Waal, Paul Burrows, Chris someone, possibly Eberts or Forest, and Skye.

Finding out who Chris is seems to me to be the priority now. Without knowing who he is, I have no idea who to look for.

I write a *'home'* alongside Joanne. I assume that's where she is. And I write the same alongside Paul.

De Waal gets a question mark, as does the name Chris.

Not in a house. Not in a house. What does that mean? I wonder.

There are a lot of possibilities. A flat? Probably not. That could be regarded as a house, and there may be too many nosy neighbours. A factory? A tent? A cabin? A caravan? Maybe a cave? What other possibilities are there?

I look on the internet for caravan parks and camping grounds in the Lismore area. There aren't many.

Staking out these would be a good way to start. But I'm not sure, not convinced. *What would I even be looking for? A man I don't know with a young girl and a woman locked up as prisoners?* I don't think so! They surely won't be that obvious.

I decide keeping two women quiet in a caravan could also be difficult. They would need to use the camp bathrooms occasionally, and such simple things would be difficult to control. *Although a lot of caravan parks have self-contained cabins, don't they?*

Think old man! Think!

As much as they could be using a factory now, during the working week that too could present a problem. Most factories are in industrial complexes. Surely the neighbours would notice?

Are there any caves around the Lismore area?

And what about a bush shack? Could that be regarded as a house?

Barry Fletcher, or Chris someone, said I shouldn't go to the police, and I've been told that I can't trust Ken Wood anyway. *So where do I go for help?*

Then I remember Leo Bryant, the man who was in charge at the local police before Ken Wood. We used to get on very well, in business and privately. I think even though he has retired, he will help, if I can find him. *It will be the old team working together again.*

I bring up the white pages directory on my computer and put in the surname, *Bryant*, Christian name, *Leo*, and the address as *Lismore*.

There is only one entry so I copy down the number and dial it.

The number answers after three rings, but I hear a recorded message. "Now that Leo has retired, we are living a life-long dream. We are now Grey Nomads. We could be anywhere in Australia. You can leave a message here and we may get it. We check occasionally." Then there was the usual *beep*.

I don't bother leaving a message. Australia is a huge country and I couldn't see Leo travelling thousands of kilometres just to possibly help me now.

A dead end.

Caves? I wonder. Are there any caves listed around the Lismore area?

I'm on my trusty internet search engine but I can't find any caves close to Lismore. It looks like there could be one near Nimbin listed on the internet, but it appears to an actual business with cave in its name. I decide, it's unlikely to be a good hiding place.

I consider places like Billen Cliffs, Lillian Rocks and Nimbin Rocks, plus all the other rocky ridges and escarpments. Surely there must be caves of some sort but if they exist, they're not listed.

Where to go from here?

Old mines or tunnels? *What about those?* I wonder.

Back to the search engine.

It looks like the nearest mining area close to Lismore is at Drake. It was an old gold mining area. But I look at

Drake on the map and decide it can't really be regarded as Lismore. It's way the other side of Casino.

I remember there has been a lot of discussion in the local papers about the old railway line from Casino to Murwillumbah. Seems half the population thinks it is recoverable, they would like to see trains running again. The other half, would appear to prefer some sort of walking or horse trail using the old railway reserve. The continual point scoring in opposing letters and articles is the type of thing which puts me off reading the local press.

Tunnels?

I find a railway engineers' report on the internet, detailing the route and the state of the old railway tracks, bridges, tunnels and culverts. From what I read, there are nine tunnels, plus a host of culverts. The two tunnels closest to Lismore are one near Bangalow and another near a place called Naughton's Gap.

Looking at a map of the railway line and the general area, the Naughton's Gap tunnel could be regarded as being in Lismore. There is really no other reasonable size town close by, except for Casino. And that's probably the same distance from the tunnel as Lismore, but in the opposite direction.

With the other tunnel being almost in Bangalow, and it being a reasonably large town in its own right, I decide that tunnel probably wouldn't be regarded as being in or near Lismore.

So, what do I now have? Two or three caravan parks, all with some sort of cabins and possibly a suitable tunnel near a place called Naughton's Gap.

Then Paul crosses my mind.

Of course! I was going to hear back from Sue about Paul's availability on Monday, but I didn't of course.

So why shouldn't I call Paul and simply act dumb.

As an old man, I actually find acting dumb fairly easy, almost natural at times.

I look at my notes and find the numbers I wrote down for Joanne Burrows. One is a mobile phone, which I assume is Joanne's personal number, and the other is a home number.

Now how do I handle it?

I decide the easiest way is to start with some truth. Tell him that I've been waiting to hear from Sue about Monday but, for some reason, she hasn't called back and she's not answering her telephone.

Then tell him I need to know his movements because I need to plan my day Monday, which will include a visit to the

213

police station to confirm whether or not I'm going to get involved in the case. I'll mention that today's Sunday but that's out because I'm spending the day with my daughter and her family.

I'll suggest, if necessary, that I'm happy to clear it with his boss if he can give me his boss's name, and somehow ask if he knows someone named Forest or Eberts.

How I can get that into the conversation, I'm not sure.

I run through it again and make notes. It all seems plausible.

Then I realize that he would, under normal circumstances anyway, tell Joanne that I called. I note *Don't tell Joanne!* Somehow I need to get that into the conversation too. Perhaps suggest that, as I haven't confirmed with her yet, it may seem unusual to her if I speak with him so soon.

I just have to play it by ear and hope for the best.

I dial the home number.

"Paul Burrows," I hear.

My turn, "Hi Mr Burrows. My name is Roy Addams. I am not sure if you've heard of me but I may be getting involved in the search for Skye."

214

"I did hear something," Burrows says. "But I thought the latest Joanne said was that you're not sure about getting involved for some reason."

Perfect, the conversation's leading as I hoped it would.

"That's quite right Mr Burrows, and I still haven't decided. But I did suggest to Joanne that perhaps I should speak to you first. And on that note, maybe you shouldn't tell Joanne I called. As I was working through her, it may put her nose out of joint if she knows I'm speaking with you. You know how women can get."

"No problem, and I know exactly what you mean. Now how can I help?" Burrows asks.

My opening?

"I want to speak with you, as soon as I can, Paul. I'm tied up today unfortunately, but I wonder if there's any chance we can catch up on Monday. I know you work, but can you find some time, preferably in the morning?"

"I guess it can be arranged, Mr Addams. Any idea how long it might take?"

"Ten to twenty minutes I think will do it. I'm trying to build a mental picture of Skye, her habits, likes and dislikes, music, movies and that sort of thing. Unfortunately Joanne seems a bit too anxious. And that's totally understandable of course.

Will it be okay with your boss if I come there?" *I'm hoping for a name.*

"Who, Chris? I'm sure he'll be fine. In fact he called this afternoon and said he needed to take a few days off, so he won't be in anyway. And the big bosses have no idea who's who or what's going on."

So, Chris whatever his name is, won't be at work for a few days. And he's Paul's boss so he knows exactly when Paul is out of the office and for how long. It seems like a perfect arrangement for Chris and Joanne.

"Tell me Paul, if you don't mind."

I need to find out about those other names, Forest and Eberts.

"Two names I've heard recently are Forest and Eberts. Do you have any idea who these people might be?"

"Hey! You sure ask some funny questions, Mr Addams. Chris is Chris Forest. Not sure why you sort of asked it out of the blue though. I thought you might've known already somehow. And Eberts? Now he's a funny one. He's related to Chris in some way, ex-brother in law or something. Anyway, John Eberts used to work for the Department, doing much the same work as me, but he was sacked about a year ago. Apparently he went out to inspect houses and, especially if the woman in the house was pretty or single, he would offer to falsify his report for sexual favours.

Two women complained and we analysed his reports for the previous year, went back and re-inspected the properties and that sort of thing. And we found these two weren't the only cases, he'd been doing it often. Chris tried to defend Eberts for a while but had to give up. There was just too much evidence against him in the end.

He's a bit of a bad bastard.

It made a few of us unpopular with Chris though, but we really didn't have much choice. We were all being watched at the time.

Anyway, water under the bridge.

I've seen Eberts around town a few times. Not sure what he's doing now, but he's definitely still around."

"Sorry if my questions seem a bit disjointed. Remember, Paul, I'm an old man and I'm just fishing for background information based on names I've heard, without any idea how they might fit together. Can I ask you another one?"

"Fire away." Paul replies.

"Would you have any idea what vehicles they both drive? Chris and this Eberts guy?"

"Wow!" Paul exclaims. "Gee, your questions really seem to come from left field. Chris drives a Department car when he can but he also has an old green Ford Falcon sedan. He drives that when he can't get the government one.

And Eberts, he's a bit of a mystery. Last time I saw him get into a vehicle it was a black four wheel drive, almost new. In fact I've seen him in it a few times but I can't help wondering how he can afford it. They're about fifty grand new.

Any other odd questions?" Paul asks.

"Mmm, just one more Paul. If you can give me your mobile number, can I call you on Monday morning to finalise a time we might be able to meet? If that's okay?"

Paul gives me his number and suggests that if he's with someone and can't answer, to just leave a message and he'll call back.

After we hung up I sit and wonder about Paul.

People had said he was a bit odd and difficult to talk with, yet I found him very friendly and cooperative. I put it down to the fact that we were speaking over the telephone and that he might perhaps be different face to face.

Ok, so now I have three caravan and cabin parks and a tunnel to watch, and two vehicles. I realise I won't be able to watch them all.

Thinking about the people involved, Janet Walsh comes to mind.

I have her telephone number somewhere.

I find the number and sit thinking, deciding how much to tell her.

I decide it's better to tell her everything, and let her decide if she wants to help, and how.

She answers the telephone on its first ring and I introduce myself.

"Mr Addams, hi." Janet says, then. "Have you heard anything? Has anything happened?"

"No, I haven't heard anything about Skye. But something has definitely happened. Are you free today and maybe tonight? And can you come and see me right away?"

"Yes, I guess I can. And I'm free today and tonight, if you think I can help. But can you tell me what's happened?"

I don't want to try to explain too much over the telephone but I know I owe her some sort of explanation. I decide to stress that I am trying to avoid the police to protect her, which is, in reality, partly true. "Janet, I think I have an idea where Skye might be, but Miss Weissman has also disappeared. And I'm worried, for both of them now.

I need help and I can't honestly think of anyone else, except for the police, but I've agreed not to contact them, to protect you. Will you help?"

"Of course I will Mr Addams," Janet says immediately. "I'll be there in half an hour or so and you can tell me your plan."

Chapter Sixteen

Janet is here within half an hour, and almost runs up the path to the front door, which I hold open for her.

Rather than beat around the bush, I explain everything from the start, including the fact that I receive my clues through spirit writing.

Unlike Sue and Joanne, Janet appears to know all about spirit writing and says she tried it several times but with no results which were decipherable. At least, she says, she couldn't understand anything which had been written. And, she says, she gathered Sue and I might have been discussing something along those lines when we were talking earlier.

The fact she knows what it's about is refreshing and saves me a lot of time defending what I had achieved so far.

I explain my discussions with Paul, the possible involvement of Chris Forest and some man named Eberts, and the fact that the spirits told me that Skye is not in a house.

I also explain my conclusions regarding a cabin with an en-suite bathroom, a bush shack, cave or tunnel, and somewhere not far from Lismore.

"Wow!" Janet says. "You have been busy Mr Addams. And I have to agree with your conclusions. What are we going to do?"

I had developed a sort of plan while waiting for Janet.

A bit hit and miss, but a plan at least.

"Janet, I suggest we both go and look for the tunnel which is the closest to Lismore, the one at Naughton's Gap. We take two cars and I'll take the lead. Once we're there, if anything happens to me, you should be able to get away and call the police. I know I said I wouldn't call them, but if things get desperate, I'm not sure we have any choice."

I am about to tell her more, when my telephone rings.

"Roy Addams here."

The voice on the other end is clear and precise.

"Mr Addams, my name is Ray Phipps and I'm with the Lismore Police Department.
Firstly, is Miss Sue Weissman with you? Or do you know her whereabouts at present?"

I tell him I have no idea where she is and that I haven't seen her for three or four hours.

Phipps continues, "I understand from Joanne Burrows that, despite you informing Inspector Wood you will probably not be involved in the Skye Burrows investigation, you have some sort of agreement with Sue Weissman that you will be involved, and effectively you already are.

Mrs Burrows says she believes you're an honest man Mr Addams but she said she doesn't trust Miss Weissman. Mrs Burrows believes that Miss Weissman engineered the abduction of Skye Burrows, in conjunction with two men, and she did it just to get some exclusive story for her paper, and to keep her job.

Now Mr Addams, I wouldn't normally discuss such a case with a member of the public but this situation is a little different because of who you are.   I'm not sure if you will remember me.

I've been at this station for a few years and I worked with you and Inspector Leo Bryant on a few cases. So I have a great deal of respect for what you do, and your unusual methods."

Ray Phipps?   Do I remember him?   The name had struck some sort of chord in the recesses of my brain when Sue Weissman first mentioned it but I couldn't recall where I might know the name from, so I didn't dwell on it.

But I remember my guides said I can trust him. And how much does he know about my methods?   I can't remember sharing them with any policemen, but I may have done.

"Umm, thank you Mr Phipps. And I understand perfectly that your calling me is unusual but I appreciate it. What do you want me to do?"

"I'll give you my number. If you hear from Miss Weissman or if you can think of anything which might help, can you please call me immediately? Any time day or night. It doesn't matter."

Phipps gives me his number and I agree to call him if I hear from Sue or think of anything new which may have some bearing on the case.

I don't tell him about the caravan park of course. If Forest and Eberts are armed, the police swooping on the caravan park could result in a blood-bath, with Skye and Sue injured or killed in the cross-fire.

"Sorry Janet. Where were we? I think I was just suggesting we should eliminate the tunnel first."

Janet nods her agreement. "Was that the police Mr Addams?"

"It was. Apparently I worked with this particular officer some years ago, but I don't actually remember him. He just said Joanne Burrows has told the police that Miss

Weissman is working with two men and that she engineered Skye's disappearance. To get an exclusive story, it appears Joanne said."

"But we know that's not true Mr Addams." Janet says. "Why didn't you tell him?"

"I know it's not true Janet. But I couldn't tell him without saying I knew Skye was with you, and I agreed not to do that."

"But now Miss Weissman is missing and probably in trouble, and the police think she's involved. That's not right!"

Janet is right of course, but I couldn't think of any way I could have told Phipps that Joanne is the problem, not Sue, without telling him all I knew, including that Janet had been hiding Skye.

"I need to do some thinking about what I tell him and how I put it. Especially if they are trying to shift the blame on to Miss Weissman. They could be planning to silence her so she can't say otherwise."

Janet looks at me wide-eyed. She agrees with my assessment of the situation.

"Now the tunnel Janet, sorry. Assuming we don't find them there, I suggest we look at the two larger caravan parks, ones which have self-contained cabins according to their advertisements anyway. If we can find suitable places, we can split up and keep watching both of the parks for a few hours. And about all we can hope to do would be to see one or both of the vehicles, an old, green, Ford Falcon and an almost new, black four-wheel drive.

If we see either of them and stay in touch, we may be in luck.

I'm not sure how we could hope to find and evaluate bush shacks. There must be thousands of them. But at least we might be able to eliminate the tunnel and the larger caravan parks reasonably easily.

Oh, and I've got some torches somewhere. I'll dig them out and we can take them with us. What do you think?"

"I guess I'm a little worried about the tunnel bit," she says. "But we won't really know how dangerous it could be until we get there and have a look at the place. So I guess I'm just being paranoid. I'm not really an outdoors type of person. The caravan parks sound pretty easy as long as we can find places to park and watch. Somewhere where we won't look too conspicuous.

What's the next step? If we can't see them at either of the places I mean?"

I shake my head. "I think it might mean back to the spirit guides from here. To see if we can get any better information."

"Wow! Great!" Janet says. "It'd be fantastic to see a professional at work."

I smile at Janet. At her enthusiasm and her naivety. I think we will make a great team, her youth and vitality and my – well, whatever it is.

I find two torches, both the large square type, supposedly water-proof. I try them and, surprisingly, they both work. The batteries seem reasonably good. But I can't remember the last time I used them.

To make sure we can locate the tunnel, I turn on my computer and get the coordinates of the Naughton's Gap tunnel from the report on the old railway. I'll plug them into my GPS when I'm in the car.

I give the basic directions to Janet, in case we get separated. Through Lismore on the main highway, right into Wilson Street then left on to Bentley Road. Look for the sign to Naughton's Gap Road and whichever of us gets to the junction first stops and waits for the other.

I explain it's only about thirty kilometres as far as I can calculate. Janet nods, all clearly understood.

We set off and I take the lead.

It's Sunday afternoon and the traffic is light, until we get to the city part of the Bruxner Highway, where it's a bit busier. At first I see Janet's car behind mine but when the highway becomes single lane, to cross the Ballina Street Bridge, she drops back a few places. I continue on Elliott Road and turn right into Wilson Street then left on to the Bentley Road, as discussed.

There are a few cars behind me but I can't see Janet's. I keep driving, find the Naughton's Gap Road junction and pull up on the side of the road. While I'm waiting for Janet, I switch on the GPS and punch in the coordinates of the railway tunnel. *I may be an old man but I just love modern technology.*

Janet pulls her car up behind mine, leaves it and joins me in my passenger's seat.

"Sorry Mr Addams but we were followed. I tried to get rid of the other car by heading up to the Nimbin Road then doubling back this way through a few side streets. I think I lost them."

"Did you notice what sort of car it was Janet?"

"I'm not real good with cars but I know it was dark green, and it wasn't a new car. In fact it looked like it may be as old as mine. And it could be the same one which picked up Skye from my place, but I can't be sure. Sorry Mr Addams. But I'm sure there was only one person in it, if that helps."

"Okay, let's just sit here for a while and I'll keep watch through the rear window."

I study the GPS screen.

"It looks like we need to turn here and drive a few kilometres along the Naughton's Gap Road, then leave the cars and walk a few hundred metres to the mouth of the tunnel."

I can't help wondering how, if the women are in the tunnel, their captors would have driven them close to the mouth. Still, I realize there are two entrances to every tunnel and the other mouth could be easier to access. And they do have a four-wheel drive.

We sit and chat for about fifteen minutes. I'm happy no other car has come along the same road so I figure Janet must have lost them.

With the basic directions clear, Janet goes back to her car and we drive to where the GPS indicates we should stop and start walking. It's late afternoon and there's still a lot of daylight left but we take the torches just in case, and lock both cars.

"Mr Addams," Janet says, sounding nervous. "Umm, we don't have any weapons. What if someone's there?"

"Janet. I'm no hero, believe me.

I don't intend getting close enough to be seen. And if I think they're in the tunnel, I'll be out of there very, very quickly and I'll call the police. I'll just tell the police I found them and you won't be mentioned. There should be no need to let them know any more than that."

"Okay. I understand. And thank you Mr Addams." Janet nods and forces a nervous smile.

I find the start of what looks like a track leading from the road, across a small hill, then down a slope. To call it a track is really overstating it. It's just an area where the grass looks like it's been bent over a few times by foot traffic. But as the GPS indicates it as a track, I assume it was used for maintenance or something, when the line was used.

I stop walking and hold my finger to my lips. I think I hear someone talking.

We walk on carefully, trying not to make a sound. The track begins to slope down and we seem to be walking along the wall of a cutting, which is just a few metres deep. As we are walking down, the hill alongside us gets higher.

We're soon at the bottom and walking on ballast, along the redundant railway lines.

The rails run round a gentle curve and I assume the mouth of the tunnel is around the bend. I motion Janet to follow me to the side of the cutting, so we can see around the bend as soon as we get there, and hopefully before anyone sees us.

Creeping closer, we hear voices, as though several men are arguing. A bottle smashes and there's laughter.

Pressed against the walls of the cutting, I can see around the bend now and the mouth of the tunnel. Janet comes closer so she can see as well.

There are four men sitting on upturned plastic crates just inside the tunnel entrance, laughing and drinking beer. After a few seconds adjusting to the surroundings, I realise they're aboriginals, and that the language they're speaking is some tribal tongue with the occasional English word mixed in, mainly swear words.

We watch and listen for about five minutes.

One finishes his bottle and throws it roughly in our direction, to laughter from the others, then gets up and urinates on the side of the track.

I decide it's time we should leave.

I wave behind me to indicate to Janet that we should head back in the direction of the cars. She doesn't need any encouragement and is soon striding along the railway lines, towards the start of the track up the side of the cutting. I struggle to keep up.

As soon as we are far enough around the bend that we can't be seen from the tunnel, Janet stops and shrugs her shoulders.

Asking me if these could be our men I suppose.

I shake my head and whisper, "no, I don't think so. Not unless they are guarding the mouth of the tunnel and there are other people inside, but there would have to be vehicles around somewhere. I think we should head for the caravan parks."

I study the ground in front of us, looking for the start of the track. The track climbs the wall of the cutting at a gentle angle and I don't want to miss it and have to scramble up the sheer cutting wall at some other point.

We find the track and begin the climb up towards the cars. At one point I stop to catch my breath. Climbing is not something I often do and, although I walk occasionally to maintain some level of fitness, it's usually, if not always, on level land.

Janet touches my shoulder. She's concerned.

"I'm fine. I don't climb often. I just need a breather."

We're soon at the cars.

"Well, that wasn't a total waste of time. If nothing else, we can eliminate that place. I can't see our guys using a place like that unless they can drive up to it and possibly into it. I don't think white guys would walk that far, just to get to somewhere quiet. And that track certainly didn't look like it had been used much recently."

"I agree," Janet says.

"Where to now, Mr Addams?"

We agree to drive into Lismore, to the closest caravan park, which is also the biggest. My plan is to find a safe parking place, somewhere that Janet will be able to see most of the park, and especially the gates, but without her car looking too conspicuous. I plan to leave her there and drive to another park, then, after a few hours, we'll switch. I'll drive to the first one and Janet will drive to the second.

The plan seems great in theory.

The first park is easy. We find a parking area on a slight rise overlooking the park. There are several empty cars parked in the area so we don't think Janet's car will look too out of place. I leave Janet there just before seven. She will call if she sees either a green Ford Falcon or a black four-wheel drive, and if I don't hear anything from her, I intend to be back around nine, to switch places.

I drive to the other park and find a good vantage point. Again there are several other cars in the area and I assume the park may restrict cars to one per site, so anyone with more than one car would be required to leave the others outside.

From where I park, I can see the main gate and most of the cabins. I regret not bringing binoculars.

I know I have a pair somewhere, but I just didn't think of bringing them.

I settle back and slide down a little so my head is level with the back of the car seat, thinking I might not be seen so easily that way.

I've been sitting in the same position for just over an hour. My back and legs are getting stiff and I know I need to get some exercise or I'll lock up.

And unlocking can get painful, as any older person knows.

As I begin to get out of the car, I hear another car pulling up at the gate, and look in its direction. It's a green Ford Falcon.

I get back into my car quickly, hoping that the other driver didn't see me as I opened my door. The interior light was only on for a few seconds, less than a minute, and it's not quite dark so the light may not have been obvious.

Also, I reason, Chris Forest, or whoever is driving the Ford probably has no idea what I look like, or what car I drive, so I'm fairly safe.

The driver reaches out and pushes some buttons on a key pad and the park gate swings open.

He pulls his arm back into the car and drives slowly along the internal road until he reaches a space between the fifth and sixth cabins.

He turns the car into the space.

The driver gets out, reaches into the back seat and takes out some bulging plastic shopping bags. Then he locks the car and walks to the sixth cabin.

Just as Chris Forest doesn't know me, I have no idea what he looks like but my instincts tells me I've found the person I've been looking for.

Now what?

Finding where Skye and Sue are held is one thing, but freeing them is something totally different. Especially as I've been told not to involve the police. And I wouldn't want to jeopardise the safety of the two women anyway, by doing anything precipitous.

I drive a few blocks and call Janet.

I suggest we meet at my house to plan what to do from here.

What to do?

How to proceed?

Surely there is some way I can turn the tables on them. I've been around a long time. I must be able to think of something!

These and other thoughts are running through my mind as I drive home.

By the time I get there, I have a plan of sorts, but a plan which will need Janet's help and cooperation, and perhaps that of some of her friends.

Chapter Seventeen

Janet's car pulls up and she parks it behind mine.

We go into the house and, like a good host should, I ask her if she wants a drink or something to eat. Not that I have a lot in the house but I feel I should offer.

She asks for a drink of water, which I bring from the kitchen, and we sit in the study.

"Okay Janet. Firstly, do you have any plans or ideas?"

"Not really Mr Addams." She admits, shaking her head. "Other than going to the police, but I know you've been trying to avoid that."

"I have, and not just for your sake Janet. I've got other reasons.

Now, I think I have a plan, and I think it might just work. Firstly, how many friends do you have with their own cars, who might be available tonight? Not for anything dangerous."

Janet thinks for a few moments. "Six or seven, maybe eight that I can think of. And two motor-bikes. Do they count?"

"Definitely! Ten or twelve vehicles, including ours will be perfect.

Now the hard part.

How do you feel about taking a note, knocking on the door of the sixth cabin and handing it to whoever answers the door?"

"I would be nervous but I'm sure I can do it, Mr Addams." But do you think just a note will do it?"

"I'm sure it won't. But it's what the note will offer which may do the trick. Also, if the cabin is surrounded by cars with their headlights trained on it, the people will know we are serious and that we have support. And hopefully it will give us the upper hand and put them on the back foot for a change.

Here, you're probably a faster typist than me. Can you take my seat and bang something out?"

I open up a new Word document and we change seats.

"Now, this is what I think we should say. If you can just type it as I say it, we can clean it up afterwards.

Hi.

We know you have Miss Sue Weissman and Miss Skye Burrows captive.

If you look outside, you will see that we have twelve vehicles around the park perimeter.

We have the place surrounded.

At this stage, these are all private vehicles. We haven't contacted the police as yet but that can be done at short notice, and our vehicles will stay in place, blocking all movement in and out until the police arrive. However, if you accept our conditions and keep to your part of the bargain, we promise we will not call the police, not immediately anyway.

The conditions are;

Within thirty minutes of receiving this note, both Miss Weissman and Miss Burrows will be set free and allowed to walk, unimpeded, to the main gate.

As soon as the two ladies are through the gate we will commence removing our vehicles.

All vehicles will be gone within fifteen minutes, but you will be free to leave the park as soon as the ladies are through the gate. We won't follow your vehicles.

We will contact the police department after the ladies walk through the gate, so you have some time to travel as far as you can, or consider some way to hide or defend yourselves.

If the ladies do not come through the gate within thirty minutes, we will move our vehicles in closer and call the police immediately. We will also have armed people on the ground to stop you if the ladies are not released and if you try to escape on foot.

There is a need for trust here, trust on both sides. On our part, it should be obvious to you that we know where you are and if we intended calling the police we would have done so already, and you would be surrounded by police cars instead of private vehicles.

If you try to make a run for it with the ladies in your vehicles, we will have up to twelve vehicles following you, and the police will be called immediately, to join in the chase.

We are offering you an opportunity to walk away and take your chances.

Should you be caught, the fact that you released the ladies of your own free will, and not under threat of police action, will, we believe, be in your favour.

Please Janet. How do you think that reads?"

"I think it's perfect Mr Addams. But how did you think of it so quickly? I mean, it seems to cover everything and I think it may just work. It offers them what is probably the only way out of this."

For some reason, I think about what Ray Phipps said about Sue Weissman being involved in Skye's disappearance, to get an exclusive story.

Janet Walsh looks at me, concerned, she can tell my mind is elsewhere.

"What is it Mr Addams? Is there another problem?" Janet asks.

She is obviously trying to read my expression.

"Just let me gather my thoughts for a moment."

My mind is wondering.

Could any of Joanne's claims be true?

Am I right in trusting Sue implicitly?

What is Sue is involved somehow?

"Janet, you remember when that policeman called earlier. He's one I think I can trust by the way.

I was thinking about what he said, that Joanne claimed Miss Weissman orchestrated Skye's disappearance, in conjunction with some men.

I know it's not the case but, well, I guess it's just left me a bit confused."

"But, but we know it's just total garbage. Firstly, Skye was with me for the first ten days or more, then when

Skye called her mother, Joanne came and collected her. Miss Weissman had nothing to do with it."

I can trust Sue. I can trust Janet. I can trust Ray Phipps. I can't trust Joanne Burrows and I can't trust Ken Wood – but can I trust what the spirits are telling me? Could I be wrong?

Could it all be wrong?

"Mr Addams! Mr Addams! Are you alright?" Janet is shaking my shoulder.

I am lost in my thoughts.

Could I have Sue and Joanne so wrong?

"Sorry Janet. I was trying to sort the chaff from the hay in my mind. And you're right. I sensed there was something wrong with Joanne from the start. Something that didn't ring true.

But listen, thinking about it again, in one way it doesn't matter what we know is true.

What really matters is what Ray Phipps believes. If he believes there's a chance Sue Weissman is involved, and he doesn't appear to know anything about Skye being with you, that means Joanne hasn't told him.

So we should be able to involve Ray Phipps in our caravan park exercise without any chance of incriminating you. He can sort out the Sue Weissman bit in his own time, but there's no way Joanne can turn around now and say she lied and that Skye was with you. So I think you're in the clear.

What do you think?"

"I see why you were thinking it over now. Not the bit about Miss Weissman, but protecting me and yet still being able to involve the police.

Thank you Mr Addams. That means a lot, and I think you're right. If Joanne hasn't told the police she knew Skye was with me, and actually collected her from my place herself, it would be impossible for her to change her story now.

Phew! It feels good to know I might be in the clear.

Are you thinking of calling the police now? I mean, despite what we put in the note?"

"What I'm thinking at the moment is that we will have our cars, plus as many of your friends as you can organise. We all meet at the park and shine our headlights on the cabin after you deliver the note.

But the note says we will be armed.

In reality, we won't be, and I don't want any of your friends to carry guns. But Ray Phipps can. If I can get him to meet us near the park, without having to explain too much before-hand, we will have someone who is allowed to be armed.

From then on, Phipps won't be able to follow both of them and deal with Skye so I think how far Forest and the other guy get is totally up to them. They should definitely have some sort of head start no matter what. Besides, when they get caught they can hardly say that it was because I didn't uphold my part of the bargain. Imagine how that would go down in court."

"Now. It's just after seven. Can you please call as many of your friends as possible and have them meet us, with their cars, just near the entrance to that caravan park. Let's say at eight thirty. That should give everyone enough time.

In the mean-time, I'll call Phipps and see if I can persuade him to meet me at eight fifteen, somewhere close, so I can explain everything to him. We need to continue with the plan and ignore this Joanne story, or rather, use it to our advantage."

"Good for you Mr A. I'm on to it. Can I take a piece of paper to make a list?"

I nod and she takes a sheet of paper and starts writing down names. People with vehicles who she thinks might be available and willing to help.

I watch her, a little jealous of her youth and vitality, and listen to the various stories she tells people to get them to cooperate. Within twenty minutes she has ten 'definites' and two more possibles.

"Now we need to check that note again, to make sure we have covered everything and print some final copies, three I think. One for you to take to the cabin, one I will keep and a third for me to give to Ray Phipps."

"Good as done." Janet says.

She prints a copy for each of us to check. Apart from two minor typing errors, we agree it's correct and says all we need to say. I suggest it should be in bold type-face, to ensure it is legible, even if the light is a bit dull.

Janet corrects the errors, changes the type-face to bold and hits the print button, while I gather up the preliminary copies, screw them up and throw them into my rubbish box.

Seven thirty and we're essentially ready to go.

"Janet, I've just thought of something else that's important.

If by any chance the man or men try to grab you when you go to the cabin, just scream as loud as you can and keep screaming. Ray Phipps and I will be with you in an instant and, with us and ten or twelve of your friends banging on the cabin, those guys will just have to give up."

"I hadn't actually thought of that." Janet admits. "Can I just threaten to scream?

"Of course you can. Hand them the note and back off immediately, saying that you'll scream the place down if they make a move towards you. That's better still.

Now, Ray Phipps."

I dial his number. I realize it's Sunday evening but he had said to call him any time.

Janet comes close so she can listen.

"Mr Phipps? Hi. Roy Addams here.

Without going into much by the way of explanation now, can you meet me in about half an hour on the corner of Wood and South Streets?

All I can tell you is that I believe I know where Skye Burrows is but because of the circumstances, I feel having a major police presence may be counter- productive and could cause the people holding her to panic and do something stupid."

He begins to say something about back-up but I interrupt him.

"Mr Phipps, Ray. If you trust me you will be there and you will be alone. If anyone else turns up I won't reveal what I know or where I think she is. I won't put her life at risk that way."

Again he begins to talk about procedures and the requirement to have mediators in place to talk with the kidnappers.

"Sorry Mr Phipps but it's my way or no way. I have taken some precautions and I believe Skye will be released without the need for any violence, on either side. And the last thing I want is for Skye to get hurt in any way. So I am going to hang up now. If we can meet at eight fifteen at the place I said, we can work on this together. Oh, and can you please bring a gun, purely as a precaution."

I hang up. Janet is looking at me wide-eyed, with her mouth open.

She closes her mouth and smiles, then, "I'm glad we're on the same side Mr Addams."

Chapter Eighteen

At eight we're on our way. Janet follows me in her car.

We park on the corner where I'm to meet Phipps and I give her directions to the park entrance and suggest where she should park to wait for her friends. As the other cars arrive, she is to direct them where to park and in which direction to point their vehicles' headlights.

At exactly eight fifteen a car pulls up next to mine. Ray Phipps gets out and joins me.

"This had better be bloody good." Phipps says, by way of a greeting.

I had sort of run through what I was going to share with him in my mind on the way here.

"Good evening Mr Phipps, and I'm sorry to drag you out on a Sunday evening but I assure you it is good.

Now, firstly, I'm going to keep the explanation as brief as I can, because we don't have a lot of time. I believe two men, Chris Forest and John Eberts, have Skye Burrows and Sue Weissman prisoners in a cabin in the caravan park just around the corner."

"What? How? How do you know that? And why Miss Weissman?"

"Later please. I will explain anything you like after this first phase is over."

I look at my watch, eight twenty two.

"In just over five minutes there will be eight to ten vehicles parked outside the caravan park, and all pointed at a specific cabin. At eight thirty a friend of mine will walk up to the cabin, knock on the door and give whoever answers it this note."

I hand him a copy of the note and switch my map reading light on.

"As my friend walks back to her car, all drivers, including us, will switch on our headlights. There will be ten to twelve, maybe more vehicles. The vehicles and lights will show the people in the cabin we are serious and that we mean business."

"Mr Addams. If you're right about this, why didn't you just come to the police? We have people who are trained in this sort of thing."

"Quite simple Mr Phipps. But we really must get going to join the others.

If the police arrived in force and surrounded the cabin, the people inside would have no way out. They would be trapped in a no-win situation, which means they could become desperate.

My way, we've given them an out. We will withdraw from the area and they will be free to drive away.

I realize now I've told you what's going on you can have police back-up here pretty quickly, but I suggest you leave calling them until we have the girls free. That way they'll think we are keeping our word and that they've at least got a chance. It should stop them doing anything stupid."

"Now I know why Inspector Bryant liked working with you Mr Addams. You've really thought this through haven't you? But why involve me at all?"

"Reading my note, you'll see I say we are armed. Actually we're not but hopefully you are. Now if they should come out with guns blazing, or try to use Miss Weissman and Skye as human shields, there will at least be some fire-power on our side. But I don't think they will. I think they'll believe what I've said in the note, let the ladies go and take their chances on the road."

"I certainly hope you're right. Now what do we do?"

I explain the basic arrangement to Ray Phipps. He goes back to his car and follows mine around the corner and into the parking area next to the caravan park.

There are already about fifteen vehicles parked outside the caravan park when we get there. Janet is directing traffic and she tells me eight are her friends. With Phipps' car, Janet's and mine, we have twelve vehicles in total, perfect.

For the first time I notice a black, almost new four-wheel drive in the car park.

Could it be John Eberts' vehicle?

I don't think it was there when I was at the park earlier, but I'm not sure.

Much as I'm tempted to let all of the four-wheel drive's tyres down, I realise that would not be in keeping with the trust aspect of our note, so I put the notion out of my mind.

Ray Phipps and I park our cars in the spaces left, then I get out and beckon Ray Phipps to join me next to Janet.

I introduce Janet to Phipps and explain she is going to deliver my note.

Janet's friend. Tony joins us and we explain what is going to happen. After Janet delivers the note, and is on her way back to the parking area, all drivers will switch their headlights on. They'll be left on until Skye and Sue leave the cabin and are at the security gate.

Then the headlights will be turned off and all vehicles will leave.

251

At least that's the plan as I explain it, and Tony goes from car to car to make sure all the drivers have the same message.

"Time to do your bit Janet, if you're ready. We'll switch our headlights on as soon as you walk away from the cabin door, so they'll know we are serious."

"Okay Mr Addams, Poppa Roy." She says, smiling at me.

She has never called me Poppa Roy before.

We all watch as Janet walks through the gate and approaches cabin six, with the typed note in her hand.

She knocks. The door opens slightly and I see a hand take the paper from Janet. Then the door is slammed shut and she immediately turns to walk away, back to the gate and the parked cars.

I shout 'lights' and all lights are switched as the message is passed along the line of cars, all directed at cabin six. Someone remembers to switch on the lights of Janet's car. Now we have eleven sets of car headlights on them.

No-one comes out of the cabin but the curtains at one of its windows are pulled aside and I see a face. The curtain is closed again.

"Poppa Roy," Janet says as she approaches my car. She sees Ray Phipps close by and motions me to one side then whispers, "Poppa Roy. I don't understand. Sue Weissman opened the door of the cabin and took the note. What's going on?"

I don't understand either.

Are Sue and Skye both captive or… I just don't have the capacity to understand?.

I put my arm around Janet. "I don't understand either. Maybe they feel they can trust Miss Weissman for some reason. Let's just wait and see what happens."

After about twenty minutes the door of the cabin opens Sue and Skye step out of the cabin into the glare of the headlights, but as they do a woman runs, screaming, from the security gate towards them. It's Joanne Burrows.

Joanne screams at Skye to get back into the cabin and shouts out how much Skye has ruined everything for her.

Sue Weissman puts her arm around Skye, whispers something to her and together they walk towards the caravan park gate.

I watch Skye and Sue and I lose sight of Joanne.

Janet and I make our way to the gate to meet Skye and Sue.

Skye is crying and Janet hugs her. Sue smiles at me. She looks as fresh and healthy as always and she holds out her arms to me. I move closer. Taking her in my arms I hug her, and hold her, wondering all the time just who or what I'm holding.

"Thank you Poppa Roy." Sue says. "I knew you'd come."

Progressively the lights of the other vehicles sweep the park as the drivers reverse and drive away, leaving just the five of us and our three vehicles. Janet and Skye sit in Janet's car and Sue joins them.

We turn the lights of our cars off so the people inside the cabin will think all the vehicles have gone.

Ray Phipps pats me on the back. "Congratulations Mr Addams. Your plan worked.

Now I know your note says you won't call the police immediately, but I will if you don't mind.

"By all means Mr Phipps, but can we then all go back to my place and talk this through? I think it will be more relaxed than the station for the ladies."

"Why not?" Phipps says. "I'm probably going to get severely reprimanded anyway for not following procedures, so one more issue can't matter. I'll get some of my people to join us, if you just give me your address."

Before Phipps gets a chance to call anyone, his telephone rings.

"Phipps here."

He frowns.

Someone is talking and he listens intently, shaking his head and shrugging his shoulders at me.

"Alright, I understand Mrs Burrows. So where are you now?

"Okay, leave it with me. We'll be with you soon."

Ray Phipps hangs up the call and smiles.

"I can see now why you warned Inspector Wood about that woman. But I have no idea how you knew she's so devious and can't be trusted.

Hang on please. Let me make few calls and I'll explain."

Ray Phipps calls a number and orders three patrol cars to come to the caravan park immediately, one to follow each of the vehicles, and he gives them the three vehicle numbers and descriptions. Joanne Burrows' car is the third vehicle.

He also asks for another car and an ambulance to be sent immediately to the Burrows house.

Phipps makes another call and organises two detectives, one man and one woman, to meet us at my house, warning them that as we're not there yet there's no need to break any speed limits.

Ray Phipps leans against his car.

"Phew, sometimes I wonder who and what I can believe in this world. Joanne Burrows told me someone broke into their house and Paul Burrows was attacked. She said she thinks it was Sue Weissman and her friends. Paul Burrows is apparently injured, possibly dying, she's not sure. And she said she's presently at a friend's house, around the corner. Oh and she said she was too upset to call an ambulance.

But she's here and Miss Weissman's here, so can I believe anything she says?"

I don't bother answering. He's really answered his own question.

Skye travels in Janet's car and Sue rides with me.

I hope they are getting their stories straight, to avoid mentioning that Skye had been with Janet.

Sue and I don't talk much on the trip, other than me answering Sue's questions about how I discovered where they were hiding, and explaining about the tunnel.

Once we're settled in my living room, Ray Phipps invites Skye to tell us what happened.

What she says is almost what Janet told us, word for word, and from what Skye says, she initially left home because of her mother's affair with Chris Forest, and stayed with an unnamed friend. Then her mother and Forest picked her up from the friend's house and took her to the cabin.

Strike one for the spirits' team I thought.

Although Phipps asks several times, Skye refuses to say whose house she had been hiding in.

Sue says that when she got to the Burrows' house, Joanne told her that Skye was in a cabin in the town and suggested they drive straight there, which they did.

According to Sue, when Joanne and Sue got to the cabin, a man opened the door, grabbed Sue and dragged her inside. The man was Chris Forest. Skye was in the bedroom of the cabin, with a rope tied from her ankle to the bed.

How was it then that Sue was not tied up as well?

And she opened the door to Janet.

I wonder, but I don't ask.

I'm not sure if I really want to know.

"So Skye," Ray Phipps summarises. "As far as your initial disappearance, you left of your own accord and stayed at some currently un-named friend's house for a few weeks?" Skye nods.

"During that time you called home to let your mother know that you were alright. Then as I understand it, you were picked up by Forest and your mother, and Forest held you a prisoner. Is that right?

"Yes Mr Phipps," Skye says. "That's exactly right."

"And when my people come you are happy to give them a statement of those facts"

"Yes Mr Phipps." Skye says.

"And just where do you fit in all of this Miss Walsh?" Phipps asks Janet.

"Skye and I talked a few times at school. And the day she saw her mother with that guy, she told me what was going on and asked my advice. I told her she should be talking to counsellors, not me. But I don't think she ever did."

Skye shakes her head.

"The next thing I heard was that Skye had been reported missing. And I heard a rumour that Mr Addams might be involved, and that he was a nice man, so I got in touch with him and told him what I knew."

"I don't suppose it occurred to you to talk to us?"

I don't think he really expected an answer to his question.

Janet just shook her head and looked away.

"And I guess you don't know where Skye was hiding before she was collected by her mother either?"

Janet shakes her head again and smiles. "No Mr Phipps, I don't. But she was with a good friend by the sound of it. Someone who tried to keep her safe."

I agree. Skye was with a very good friend for a few weeks. From what little I know of the situation, they had become friends and Janet had tried to keep her safe. Perhaps Janet had made a mistake in insisting Skye call her mother when she did. But Janet would have done it with the best of intentions. I'm convinced of that and I just hope Joanne doesn't say too much about where Skye had been. But I guess, after all the lies Joanne has obviously told, people probably won't believe her anyway. I certainly hope they don't.

While I'm lost in my thoughts, the other police officers, a man and a woman, arrive.

Ray Phipps introduces them and tells us that, in accordance with standard police procedures, each of us will be interviewed individually, and statements prepared.

He asks if they can use my dining room for the interviews, and if the room can be closed off from the other rooms. I assure him it can and that the walls and doors are quite solid so conversations won't be overheard.

The police woman asks Skye to go into the dining room with her.

Sue Weissman smiles at me and raises one eyebrow.

I gather she is trying to ask me a question, I think perhaps about how much she should say about my mumbo jumbo, but perhaps I'm wrong.

I decide to cover that possibility, to try to make it easier for her to answer any questions about my methods.

"Mr Phipps, if I'm right, you know a little about my methods. I mean the way I find information and clues?"

Phipps clears his throat. He looks at the other policeman, then replies. "Yes Mr Addams, I do. I'm not sure I believe all of it but when we worked together before, Inspector Bryant explained your, well let's call them your procedures. Do you want to make a statement now?"

I shake my head.

Both Janet and Sue are in the room and both know how I operate. I hope what I say will make things easier when it's their turns to be interviewed.

"Actually I don't want to make a statement at all. All I will say is that my method gave me suggestions, who to trust, who not to trust and that sort of thing. And where to look, very rough hints, which Janet and I followed up. And Miss Weissman was here during one of my, well, my procedures, and assisted me with questions and in interpreting the answers.

Without any doubt, these two ladies helped me, in different ways, and I can appreciate they may have trouble explaining this when they are interviewed. Whatever they tell your associate may sound like, well, like mumbo jumbo, which is why I'm telling you now. As for the rest, if you remember my methods I have absolutely no idea where the information comes from, which is why I just can't make an official statement."

Sue Weissman smiles at me and nods. I decide I was right; *she would have had difficulty explaining her role and my methods.*

Janet is smiling as well and I hope I've made it easier for her to answer any questions the officers may have.

261

Ray Phipps looks at the other officer and shakes his head. "I know what Mr Addams just said probably won't make sense but let it go. I'm happy there is no need for us to take an official statement from him."

The other officer looks confused but doesn't say anything.

Skye comes out of the dining room and tells Janet the female officer is waiting for her. I notice Skye squeezes Janet's hand as they pass each other and smiles. I assume it to be a signal that her statement is as discussed earlier and that Janet isn't mentioned.

Janet is out after just a few minutes, which is appropriate if her role was simply helping me for the last twenty-four hours or so.

I'm not sure how Janet explains why she didn't go to the police, or how she heard about me, but as I've refused to make an official statement, I decide it is irrelevant.

Sue Weissman is in the dining room with the female officer for a lot longer.

When Sue comes out, Ray Phipps asks the other officers to organise transport for Sue, Skye and Janet, then asks me to join him in the dining room for a quiet, unofficial, chat.

"Mr Addams, I have no idea how you get your information and honestly, I don't care. It seems to work and that's all that matters to me.

There are a few things which intrigue me though."

He is studying my face, looking for a reaction I suppose.

"How did you know we should look at the CCTV tapes outside of the main Shopping Centre? I mean, how could you have possibly known, when my team missed them completely?"

That was an easy one.

"Pure luck Mr Phipps, I assure you. I didn't know. I've gone into the centre that way myself and I simply remembered that entrance when Miss Weissman told me there was nothing on the car-park CCTV's."

"And what would you say if I told you the girl with Skye, on one of the tapes at least, looks a lot like Janet Walsh?"

Now the questions are more like I would have expected.

"Mr Phipps, I suggest it's purely a coincidence and recommend that particular tape should disappear. It has no bearing on the abduction case, does it?"

Phipps nods, "I thought that would be your answer. I know I shouldn't, but I agree with you, totally."

"Now my last question, well the last one I think I might get a straight answer to. When I told you that Joanne Burrows complained that Miss Weissman engineered the whole thing, and that she, Miss Weissman had abducted Skye with two accomplices, you seemed to know that wasn't true. That Joanne Burrows was lying. How could you know that?"

Ah, how did I know anything?

I decide to keep the information simple.

"It's easy actually Mr Phipps. As I said earlier, my mumbo jumbo tells me who I can believe and trust, and who I can't.

I just believed what I was told."

Chapter Nineteen

Skye and Janet are leaving as Ray Phipps and I come out of the dining room.

At Skye's request, the police allow her to go home with Janet, subject to her agreeing to attend the police station on Monday morning to talk with a youth counsellor.

The young ladies are beaming and they both give me a hug as they leave.

Sue is the next to leave.

The police woman offers to drive her home.

Sue kisses me on the cheek and squeezes my arm as she leaves. "Thank you Poppa Roy," she says. Then she's gone.

I hadn't noticed but Phipps was looking around the house and he's in my study. He comes out with some sheets of paper in his hand. "Is this how you contact your friends and get your information?"

I just nod and smile. "Not the sort of thing you can use in evidence though I'm afraid."

Ray Phipps laughs and shakes his head.

Chapter Twenty

It's Monday morning and I'm up early.

Phipps calls and tells me they picked up John Eberts. His car was stopped at a police road-block on the Pacific Highway near Taree, four and a half hours after we left the caravan park.

The patrol car and ambulance were at the Burrows house in time to save Paul Burrows, but his condition is still listed as critical. When they found him he was on the floor with a knife stuck in his chest. Phipps says Paul had lost a lot of blood and he's unconscious and on life support so the police were unable to question him.

Despite the police road-blocks and check-points, which were in place less than an hour after Skye and Sue walked out of the caravan-park, somehow Joanne Burrows and Chris Forest had managed to escape.

In Ray Phipps' opinion, they were holed up somewhere in Lismore or nearby. The other possibility is that they travelled on very minor roads rather than main highways, to avoid the police. But Phipps believes this to be less likely.

"Mr Addams," Ray Phipps says, sounding a little sheepish. "I know this may sound like a strange request, and that I'll be in serious trouble if anyone here finds out, but can you use your powers to find out where they are? I mean, can it work that way? Can you ask a direct question and hope to get an answer?"

It was my turn to laugh, a little laugh.

"Mr Phipps, I appreciate your trust and I'd be delighted to try. But as long as you understand there are no guarantees, and the information I receive may not be easy to interpret.

Incidentally, do you have someone checking on Miss Walsh and Miss Weissman? Also on

Paul Burrows? If it was Joanne or Forest who stabbed him, they might have another go. To stop him talking."

"You're right of course Mr Addams, and yes, I think we have them all covered. There's a permanent guard at the hospital and we have contacted both Miss Weissman and Miss Walsh.

They are both home and Skye is still with Miss Walsh. We have a car outside each of their homes, and the cars will stay there until I say otherwise.

Oh, and there's also a car in your street.

If you look out of your window you'll see a white Camray with two people in it. That's us.

Now, what about your mumbo jumbo Mr Addams?"

"Do you have any idea what questions you want me to ask?"

"Hell no! I don't. I honestly have no idea. I guess the easiest would be to ask where they are, but I don't suppose it's that simple."

"Normally, no. It isn't that easy. I can ask that sort of question but often I won't get a logical answer.

Unfortunately, the questions which seem to get the best results are the more abstract, less definitive ones, such as *have they left Lismore? Are they close? Are they hiding in a house? Are they threatening anyone? Have they hurt anyone?*

It's almost a case of posing every question such that it needs only a *yes* or *no*, or a one word response, where possible. These seem to work much better. I understand it's similar with Ouija boards."

"Mr Addams, we don't have time for Ouija boards. Can I leave it with you please? To do what you can. And can you do something today? This morning?"

"What about Inspector Wood? What does he say about my being involved?"

"Mr Addams, I'm already up to my neck in trouble because of last night and the fact I didn't follow standard procedures and call for back-up. I have no idea how it will end up for me but Ken Wood is not happy that Mrs Burrows and that Forest guy got away.

I told him what I had in mind a few minutes ago, about calling you I mean, and he hit the roof. He did at first anyway. Then he relented a little, but told me, in no uncertain terms, that it's totally on my head. Basically, if the outcome isn't positive, as far as he's concerned I can kiss my career good-bye."

I appreciate how much Ray Phipps is sticking his neck out by putting his trust in me and my mumbo jumbo, much further than he might have been over last night.

"And you're still willing to take that risk?"

"Honestly, I can't see that we have a choice Mr Addams. As I see it, you're our only hope. I believe you can see where others can't, and I think that's exactly what we need at the moment.

Can we count on you?"

I find it an interesting question. I'm not even sure I can count on me a lot of the time. But I've grown to like Ray Phipps.

"Mr Phipps, Ray, you can count on me to try. Beyond that I just don't know. But I don't want to talk to anyone else

269

in the department. As far as I'm concerned, we're working on this together and I'm doing this as a favour for you. Is that okay with you?"

"Perfectly, and thank you Mr Addams. Umm, can I ask how long will it take?"

The 'how long is a piece of string' question comes to mind, but I think I can do better than that. I seem to usually be away somewhere for around two hours, so, allowing an hour to prepare and to decipher any results, I think around three hours should be adequate.

"Mr Phipps, it's almost ten now. I'll call you between one and two today. It may be sooner but I can't always control these things, so three to four hours overall is my best guess."

We finish the call.

I know he's a bit disappointed I don't say I'll call back sooner, but he doesn't say anything. From what he has said I understand he's under a lot of pressure, but, as much as I like the man and want to help, I can't take his pressure on as my own. It just doesn't work that way.

I unplug the telephone and go into my study.

Chapter Twenty-one

I find my note pad and plan my questions. Like before, I write a short preamble, explaining who Joanne Burrows and Chris Forest are.

My simple logic is that, although I've asked questions concerning both Burrows and Forest previously, I have no idea if I'll be in contact with the same spirits, if in fact it is some sort of external presence. So, by explaining all, I consider I'm giving myself the best chance of getting answers.

My questions are, I hope, pretty straightforward.

Is Joanne Burrows still in Lismore?

Is Chris Forest still in Lismore?

Are they together somewhere?

Are they in a house?

Is Skye Burrows in danger?

Is Sue Weissman in danger?

Is Paul Burrows in danger?

Are they close to me?

Are they threatening someone?

Is that person in danger?

Do I know that person?

Have they hurt that person?

Can I find them?

Who can help me find them?

Will they hurt someone?

Will the police catch them?

I read through the questions a few times. I'm not sure I can ask anything else, other than a direct question about their whereabouts, which I avoided because I didn't expect they would give me a direct response.

Expecting the worse, I write down the question anyway.

Where are Joanne Burrows and Chris Forest?

Double-spaced, the questions take up most of my page. I tape the page to my desk and clear away all the other papers and blank pads.

It's ten thirty by the time I open up my mantra and try to concentrate. This time I select a different mantra, a very plain one which I know is Indian, and I study the shapes and forms.

Many of them appear to be of animal and flowers, unlike the other mantras where the shapes are purely geometric.

It doesn't seem to take long and I am aware I've gone somewhere else.

oOo

I look at the clock.

It's almost twelve thirty. Again I've been elsewhere for around two hours.

I often think I'd like to find out why it's usually around two hours and if I can change it, or control it. But I have no idea where to start.

There is some more writing on my sheet of questions. I cut the sheet from the desk and examine it closely. As usual there are a lot of letters which may be meant to form words, but they are not words I can interpret.

Perhaps some are another language. I had never really considered that possibility previously.

As is my usual practice, I initially try to match the responses closest to the questions, with the questions.

Is Joanne Burrows still in Lismore?

??YES

Is Chris Forest still in Lismore?

273

??YES

Are they together somewhere?

??YES

From the first three responses I believe they are together, and they are still somewhere in or near Lismore.

Are they in a house?

YES

Is Skye Burrows in danger?

~~**YES**~~**/NO**

Is Sue Weissman in danger?

~~**YES**~~**/NO**

I interpret the 'yes,' then 'no' to indicate both Skye and Sue could be in danger but not directly, or imminently.

Is Paul Burrows in danger?

POOR PAUL

PAUL IS NO MORE

Are they close to me?

??????

I understand that again my question is probably too ambiguous, not specific enough in my definition of 'close.'

Are they threatening someone?

YES

Is that person in danger?

274

YES

Do I know that person?

YES

Have they hurt that person?

YES

I assume the responses mean they are holding someone hostage, probably in their own home, and that the person is someone I know, but who?

I've known a lot of people over the years.

I think I know from the previous answers it's not Sue or Skye, but that doesn't narrow it down by much.

Can I find them?

????YES

Who can help me find them?

?????

Will they hurt someone?

??????

Will the police catch them?

??????

Where are Joanne Burrows and Chris Forest?

NOT FAR

YOU KNOW

Somehow I should know where they are, or so my writing tells me.

I'm confused.

I turn the sheet of paper around and look for upside down words and any written backwards amongst the scribble. Then I see it!

ASIL

Lisa! They are at Lisa's house!

Of course!

Fletcher or Forest or whatever his name is, called Lisa to try to get me to avoid the case. He must have known her married name to get her number in the first place, and yes, she's in the local directory, as Sue had suggested earlier.

I scramble for my telephone and plug it into the wall socket. There are no messages.

I dial Ray Phipps, calling his mobile number. It's twelve fifty-five, a little sooner than I had anticipated.

He answers. "Phipps here."

Mr Phipps, Ray. It's Roy Addams here. Firstly, is Paul Burrows dead?

The line is quiet, then. "Not that I am aware Mr Addams. What have you heard?"

"Heard? Nothing. But my writings say '*Poor Paul*' and '*Paul is No More.*' How long since you have checked? I mean, could my message be right? I need to know because if it's right, I will assume the rest of the messages are right."

"Hang on. I'll check on the other line."

I can hear a conversation, it seems there is no news but I hear Phipps asking someone to go immediately and physically check Paul Burrows. The line is silent.

Then I hear. "Thank you. Please submit a report as soon as possible."

Phipps finishes the other call.

"Mr Addams, I have no idea how you do what you do but you're correct. Paul Burrows died from his injuries, and it's estimated he died in the last hour and a half. That's when he was last checked. I've been having them doing a physical check every two or three hours, hoping he may regain consciousness enough to talk to us.

What else can you tell me?"

"Joanne and that guy are alive and in Lismore. They're holding someone in their own house and, well, I believe it's Lisa, my daughter.

But I can't be sure. It could be a different Lisa.

The reason I think it's my daughter is that Forest called her earlier and told her to warn me off getting involved in the case. So I am assuming they got her details from the directory. The address is 30 Evans Street, in Goonellabah."

"We're on the way Mr Addams. And what is her married name, by the way?" Ray Phipps asks.

"And I'm on my way too Mr Phipps, as soon as we finish this call. Her name is Carthew, Lisa Carthew. And it's only because of me she's in this mess. I'm not sure what I can do but I want to be there."

"And I wouldn't even think of trying to suggest otherwise. I know I'd be wasting my breath. But please stay clear of the house until we know what's going on. We'll meet you there."

Stay clear of the house! What a silly request. I'll do whatever I can to protect Lisa. And the kids if they're home.

Chapter Twenty-two

I head out slowly.

I'm driving more carefully than I would normally, but my mind is racing. What if's seem to fill it, but with no answers.

Do I rely on the police?

Can I?

Will they go in with guns blazing?

How can I, or we, make sure no-one is hurt?

Suddenly it's like a light going on somewhere. There is a burst of inspiration and I'm sure I have the answer.

But will Ray Phipps and his cronies agree?

I turn the corner into Lisa's street. There is a police car parked across the road, blocking my way, and two other police cars parked between that one and Lisa's house. And I can see more police cars blocking the street from the other side.

The police certainly got here quickly.

I leave my car as close as I can and get out, looking around for Ray Phipps. I can't see him but a policeman at the road block calls him on a radio. I see a hand wave from behind one of the other vehicles and a message comes through the radio to let me through.

I make my way carefully to the other car, staying well away from the houses on Lisa's side of the street.

Ray Phipps gestures for me to crouch lower, behind the parked car. He's there with two plain-clothed male officers and a woman in uniform.

"What do you know at this stage?" I ask. " Are they in there and are they armed?"

"They're definitely in there. We've been on the telephone to them, via Lisa's number. They say they have Lisa and her eldest son, Michael.

The younger children were allowed to leave earlier and they're with a neighbour. Or so Lisa told us before they took the telephone away from her.

That Forest guy says they've got a rifle each, but we really have no idea if he's telling the truth. No shots have been fired, but we're not taking any chances.

So far there haven't been any demands and we have no idea what they want."

"Do you have a plan?"

I think it's a fair question, under the circumstances.

"Our plan at the moment is to just wait them out. With no demands and no obvious threats, it's hard to determine what else to do.

I've got an expert negotiator on the way, so hopefully we can get them to surrender without any blood-shed.

I probably shouldn't ask Mr Addams, but I suppose you have a plan?"

"Yes I have, as a matter of fact. Working on the likelihood they believe I've caused all their problems, I'd like to offer to take Lisa and Michael's place."

"You mean you go in and they come out, something like that?"

"Precisely that. Because I'm the one who identified them and obviously led the police to them, at the park and here, they must see me as a continuous threat, no matter where they go.

And, because of that, I hope they'll see me as being a more valuable hostage than a mother and son."

"But Mr Addams, damn it, what you're saying is the very reason I can't agree to an exchange. Without you out here, we honestly have no method of tracing them. You're the only reason we know where they are now for Christ's sake. Sorry but I can't agree with it."

I look at Ray Phipps, then at his fellow officers. They've been quiet during our exchange.

"Ray, I think you know me pretty well by now, well enough to realize there is more to my plan than my just walking in there.

But I can't share the details with you, if you don't mind. It has to come as a surprise, to them and to you.

Regardless, I want you to call them and offer a swap. Now please, before I change my mind. Otherwise I might just stand up, walk across the street and knock on Lisa's door."

Ray Phipps looks at my face, then at his watch. It's just after three.

"I'll make a deal with you Mr Addams.

I think the negotiating team is on its way, at least that's what I've been told.

If they're not here by three thirty, we'll do it your way. And yes, I'll be sticking my neck out again, but I think we all agree, one hour for the team to get here and take some action is reasonable. Any longer than an hour with those idiots inside would be expecting too much of Lisa and Michael."

The policewoman smiles and nods. "I agree sir. The others should be here by now and we haven't heard a thing from them."

282

I really have no idea of her rank or what authority she might have in these circumstances, but I'm glad she's supporting Ray Phipps' decision. It should result in the decision being regarded as a team effort, and not just Ray Phipps acting as a lone gun.

We wait.

My legs aren't what they used to be and I have trouble staying crouched so I roll forward on to my knees. I know I'll probably have a terrible time straightening up, but I accept we need to keep down, especially if they have rifles.

Half an hour can seem like hours when you're waiting for something, and it does now.

I keep looking at my watch but the hands move so slowly. It's frustrating

Finally Ray Phipps nods. "That's long enough. I'll call them and suggest an exchange in the middle of the street. Or at the front gate. Somewhere we can keep an eye on all of you."

"Before you do, can someone help me up please? My old knees tend to lock up, especially the left one."

Ray Phipps stands and helps me to my feet. My left

knee has locked a little. I rub it to try to stimulate it back to life, and flex it a few times.

Phipps has the telephone to his ear, waiting for someone in the house to pick it up.

"Hello, Detective Phipps here again. Is that Mrs Burrows?

Okay.

Mr Roy Addams is out here with us. He would like to make sure his daughter and grandson are safe and he's offering himself in exchange for them.

Yes, that's right. He'll join you in the house if you release Lisa and Michael."

Ray Phipps appears despondent as he looks at the silent telephone.

"The line just went dead. I think she hung up on me."

"I guess it's a fairly big decision and she needs to talk it through with Forest," I suggest.

The others nod.

The telephone rings and Phipps answers.

"Hello, yes this is Detective Phipps. What we suggest is that Mr Addams will cross the road and walk up to the front door, but he will stand aside until Lisa and Michael come out. That way you will basically have him there while the exchange takes place. He will actually enter the house after they come out.

Trust us? Of course you can trust us. He'll be with you there anyway, perhaps outside the door until they come out, but there with you. And he's an old man. He's hardly going to break into a sprint and run away."

Ray Phipps shrugs his shoulders and raises his eyebrows to me as he says the last bit, perhaps as a sort of apology I guess. But I realize he doesn't really have much choice. He has to say whatever it takes and it's not far from the truth anyway. I could hardly make a dash for it, and possibly end up with a couple of bullets in my back for my trouble.

"They've agreed." Ray Phipps says, finishing the call. "If you're near the front door in ten minutes, they'll let Lisa and Michael out and you go in. I still don't like it Mr Addams. I don't trust them."

"I don't like it either Mr Phipps. But I can't leave a mother and her young son in there, whether they're my relatives or not. Besides, it's a nice day for a walk across the road."

My left knee is functioning quite well now and there doesn't seem to be any pain. I flex it a few more times to make sure I can walk without it hurting.

I look at my watch. Only three minutes have gone but I decide I am going across the road anyway. I'll just wait outside the door.

"I am off Detective Phipps. Please make sure Lisa and Michael are looked after, and remind Michael about black, white and grey. He should know what you mean."

Ray Phipps and the others stand. They shake my hand and wish me luck.

I look around the quiet street. At the road-blocks either end, small groups of people have gathered and I see a tall blonde figure waving vigorously. It's Sue Weissman.

I've still got a few minutes, and not knowing exactly what might happen or if I will ever see her again, I walk over to the road-block and explain to the uniformed officer that I need to talk to someone and then come back. He lets me past.

Sue comes to me and we hold each other.

"Poppa Roy, why didn't you call me? What's going on?

I explain very quickly, that they have Lisa and Michael hostage in the house and I'm on my way to exchange myself for both of them.

"Oh Roy. Please be careful. We've really only just met and I'd hate it if anything happens to you now."

She hugs me again and kisses me on the cheek. She has tears in her eyes. I hold her tight then turn away, and walk towards Lisa's house, with tears welling in my eyes.

Chapter Twenty-three

I'm no hero. I've never sought fame, or even recognition and I've always been happy in my anonymity, my reclusion.

But there is an enormous sense of personal pride as I walk towards Lisa's house, pride that I am about to do something to help save my family. I know the police and people behind the barricades are watching me, and I have no doubt pictures are being taken, which will probably appear in the Globe, and other papers.

I find that aspect a little annoying, unnerving, maybe even daunting, but I know it sort of goes with the territory. When you do something people see as heroic, you must expect to be seen as something of a hero.

Otherwise don't do it, or don't be seen doing it. I don't think I really have too much choice. It's mid-afternoon and everyone in the area can see me.

Oh well, I made the decision, now I have to live with it and all it entails.

Across the road, through the front gate and up the path to the front door. It's not far and it only takes about two minutes, but it's probably one of the longest and loneliest walks of my life.

The curtains are open and I see shapes inside. Faces perhaps. I try not to look too intently. I don't want to see anything which might put me off from my quest.

I'm not sure what to do when I reach the door so I just knock then stand back a few paces. The door opens slowly and Michael comes out.

It's obvious he's been crying, but he smiles bravely and hugs me.

"Poppa Roy, thank you for coming to get us."

I'm not sure he's aware that I'm going into the house to take his place. They may not have told him. But I don't say anything either.

Then Lisa comes out. She's crying. I put my arms around her.

"Oh dad. Thank you. I love you dad. I don't really know what else to say. You're so brave, and generous, but please be careful."

"Have they hurt you Lisa? Or Michael?"

"No dad, they haven't. Not physically anyway, but I think I'm a total wreck emotionally. I don't know how much longer I could have lasted. Not knowing is the worst part. Not knowing what they might do."

"Mr Addams! Inside now please." It's an instruction from someone whose voice I don't recognise, Chris Forest I assume.

I hold Lisa for a few moments then let her go and she and Michael walk away, towards the waiting police officers.

I walk into the house.

Most of the curtains are drawn and the room is half dark but I can clearly see Joanne Burrows sitting on a chair, crying, and a man standing next to her, holding what looks like a twenty two calibre rifle.

"Close the door please, Mr Addams." Forest says. "And come in and sit down."

I do as instructed.

I sit opposite Joanne. She looks at me then looks away and lowers her head. "I'm sorry Mr Addams. I didn't mean for any of this to happen. Everything has just gotten out of hand."

"Shut up Joanne. That's not helping." Forest says fiercely. "Mr Addams. I let you come in here in exchange for your daughter and grandson for one reason only. I figure you've spent some time with the police out there and you might have some idea what they are planning and how we can get out of this."

In the dim light I can't see his face clearly but I gather he is serious.

It's time for me to play my role and lie a little.

"Mr Forest, Mrs Burrows. I didn't come in here with the intention of helping you escape. Sorry if you think otherwise.

Basically I'm an old man. I've lived a good life and enjoyed most of it and, as far as I'm concerned, I'm here to take whatever consequences you or the police decide to deal up. If they come in guns blazing, so be it.

I decided I'm on the downhill slope anyway with my angina and blood pressure problems, so my life is pretty well limited. And that's the only reason I offered to be here, so Lisa and young Michael could live out their lives as I've lived mine.

I'm sorry if I disappoint you, but I'm ready to die with you if that's the way this has to end."

Joanne burst out crying again, louder this time.

Forest mutters a few things. I'm not sure what he says but I think I hear the words 'stupid,' 'idiot' and 'bitch,' so I gather my coming in was Joanne's decision.

Time for the next phase of my plan.

"Sorry Mr Forest, but do you mind if I lie down somewhere, perhaps Michael's room. I think the stress of all this is getting to me and I feel a bit faint."

I don't wait for an answer but stand up, making it look like I'm doing it with difficulty.

Joanne is immediately concerned, something I was relying on. "Go ahead Mr Addams. What can we do to help?"

"Can I have a glass of water please?"

I reach into my pocket and take out some tablets. Actually they're just aspirin, something my doctor prescribed years ago which I haven't bothered taking, but which I seem to always have with me for some reason.

Perhaps this is the reason. Who knows why these little coincidences occur?

Phase three, and hopefully my plan will work as I envisaged.

Taking the glass of water, I make a show of taking the tiny tablets and, without waiting for their approval or permission I shuffle my way to Michael's room. Joanne watches from the doorway as I lie on the bed and turn so I am facing away from her. I'm relying on her being a caring and decent human being at heart.

Facing the wall, I close my eyes and try to conjure up my favourite mantra. I try to remember it in precise detail, all the shapes and the different colours.

Yes, I see it. It is real and I study it more, counting shapes and blending colours.

Then I go somewhere else.

Chapter Twenty-four

When I come back to reality I understand my trust in Joanne is justified.

I am on a bed.

People are fussing around me and there is an ambulance next to me.

Someone says they are ready to take me to hospital.

"Thank you, but that won't be necessary. I'm fine."

I sit up, swing my legs off of the bed and stand. There is a crowd of people around me including police and others dressed in hospital garb.

"Oh dad. Thank goodness you're alright." Lisa is crying as she and Michael come closer and hug me.

"When Joanne called we thought you'd had a massive heart attack or something."

"And what did you think Michael?" I ask, smiling.

"I remembered what you said about black, white and grey, after the policeman told me I should, and I sort of realized things might not be what they seem. But I wasn't sure how and I was worried too."

Ray Phipps comes into sight, Sue Weissman is with him. Sue is crying and she pushes past Phipps and Lisa, not caring who sees her or what they think of her.

Ignoring everyone, Sue hugs me and kisses me, a few times.

"You old bugger. You had me really worried this time. I didn't know what to think."

"Mr Phipps." I say, turning to the policeman, "Where is Joanne Burrows?"

"She's in the back of that police car over there. We were just about to take her into the station."

"Can I talk to her please?"

Ray Phipps nods and I walk over to the car he had indicated. A policeman moves to stop me as I open the rear door but Ray Phipps nods in his direction and I'm face to face with Joanne again.

"You're okay? Joanne asks, tears streaming down her cheeks. "I thought you were gone and I didn't want that on my conscience as well as all the other stuff. We thought it was a massive heart attack, or maybe a stroke, the way your right hand kept twitching and moving. As if it was looking for something."

"I'm fine Joanne. It was just a trick I decided to play.

I just want to tell you that I was relying on you being a decent human being, and I was right. And I'll do whatever I can to make sure the authorities realize you did the right thing in the end. Thank you for that."

Walking back towards the others I see Ray Phipps looks a little stern.

"You could have told us what you had planned Mr Addams. We were all worried. Honestly, I thought I was responsible for sending you to your death or something."

"Sorry Inspector. I told you I wouldn't tell you the details of my plan. And I didn't say anything for that very reason. It had to be believable, to you and everyone else, for it to work. Everyone had to panic. Otherwise they would have suspected something was wrong."

"Sue Weissman is right. You are an old bugger. A cunning old bugger. And I'm glad we're on the same team."

o0o

The police had stormed the house when they heard a shot.

The shot was fired when Joanne and Chris Forest struggled for the gun. Joanne wanted to call for an ambulance and surrender, when she thought I'd had a heart attack, but Forest didn't. He had been prepared to let me die and still hoped to find a way to escape.

When the police broke the front door down the gun and Forest were on the floor and Joanne was standing over them.

Forest was shot in the foot when the gun went off during the struggle, but he was otherwise okay.

No-one knew what to make of my condition, no- one except perhaps young Michael.

Chapter Twenty-five

Sue and I haven't really talked much about the details of the Skye Burrows case.

I decide I don't need to know how it was that she was the one who opened the cabin door, or what involvement she might have had, if any.

I wonder about Skye Burrows and Janet Walsh too, but in a more positive way. Skye is living with her aunt on the other side of Lismore and I see her from time to time. She told me she intends moving in with Janet when she's a little older. With Paul gone, and Joanne in prison, Skye will have the family home. But Janet has told me that Skye will probably sell the house and that the two of them will travel somewhere, and I wished her, and Skye all the luck in the world.

Sue's stories in the Globe were picked up by the national dailies and she rode on the crest of the media wave for a few months.

Yes, I sometimes wonder.

I think about Skye, Janet and Sue, but when I look at Sue now, sleeping peacefully in my bed, I know there are some things I just don't need to know.

In the overall scheme of things, they don't matter. The world keeps turning and day still follows night.

About the Author

R. Addams (Poppa Roy) has been a resident of the Northern Rivers region of New South Wales in Australia for the last three years.

Prior to relocating to this idyllic location, the author lived in Adelaide, Melbourne and Perth, and managed large multi-disciplined construction projects in many areas of Australia, Qatar, Bulgaria and Ghana, West Africa.

The author has travelled extensively throughout Australia and has visited many other countries including most states of the USA, approximately ten countries in Europe, three in Africa and numerous countries in Asia, the South Pacific and the Caribbean.

R Addams lives with his wife of forty-seven years.

Their daughter and three grand-children live in the same town and their son, and two more grand-children live in Perth, Australia.

R Addams and Poppa Roy are pseudonyms.

Also by R Addams

Chaloaw Stew – ISBN 978-0-9943452-1-9

Published by Smashwords June 2015

CHALOAW STEW

(Nothing Ever Happens in Alstonville)

A Novel by R. Addams

Chaloaw Stew is a crime thriller set in the Northern Rivers region of northern New South Wales, Australia.

It is a rough and raw account of young female back-packers who are picked up by an unscrupulous gang of deviates

The local police have no clues and when their investigation stalls, two Sydney detectives are assigned to the case, Rick Lorenzi, a seasoned vice professional and Chris Johnson.

Chris is a young and attractive blonde, with experience specifically in crimes against women. Also, Chris has developed a system of criminal categorization, similar to profiling. She is a crack shot and a martial arts specialist, and can hold her own in what is still very much a man's world.

Chaloaw Stew follows the police investigation, led by Rick and Chris, and the sometimes unorthodox methods employed to track down the culprits, with some totally unexpected twists towards the end.

Whereas Seeking Skye may be described as "cute and cozy," Chaloaw Stew is anything but. It is hard-hitting and gruesome in places and is definitely not for the faint-hearted.

R Addams

Acknowledgements

All authors have peers whose valued opinions and comments are appreciated, and I am no exception.

Thanks, in particular to Ian Green (Melbourne, Australia), James Hudson (East Ballina, Australia) and John Liddi (Silver Springs, Maryland, USA) for their encouragement and constructive (usually anyway) comments and suggestions.

Thanks also to Lynda Lovett for her untiring support and her fine effort in editing the final manuscript.

Unlike Poppa Roy's, my wife is very much alive and has been a tower of strength, putting up with my self-imposed reclusion at times. And my daughter, she is definitely the total opposite of Lisa, Poppa Roy's daughter. My daughter is understanding, tolerant and non-judgmental, and has been totally supportive.

Thanks also to my son for his comments and encouragement, and my wider family and close friends who have continually supported my efforts.

R Addams

Disclaimer

This novel is a work of fiction and (with a few exceptions); all characters' names are created by the author, without reference to any person, living or deceased.

[In a few instances, names of friends have, with their express approval, been included in the work.]

Any similarity between the other names used in this work and those of actual people is purely coincidental.

The locations mentioned in this work are real but there is no suggestion that similar events ever took place in these locations.

The novel mentions Automatic, Spirit or Magic Writing, as a means by which I obtain clues to help me solve cases. In reality, I have no first- hand knowledge of Spirit Writing. While I do not claim that it works or that it is reliable, neither do I de-bunk or attempt to discredit what may well be a reliable method of a form of spiritual communication.

A copy of the description of Automatic Writing in Wikipedia is included, for information only.

R Addams

Automatic Writing/Spirit Writing

There are various terms used to describe the phenomena of writing sub-consciously. Although I don't profess to have the ability myself, over the years I have been aware of people who have, or who claim they have.

When creating Poppa Roy, I decided to add a degree of mysticism by giving him the ability, executed in the manner in which it was described to me by an individual some years ago.

This person called it "Magic Writing," and I suggest this is as good a term as any.

Seeking Skye is of course a work of fiction, and it is not claimed to be anything other than that.

The following are some words from Wikipedia, on the subject (for information only).

R Addams

From Wikipedia (Hyperlinks have been deleted)

'Automatic writing as a spiritual practice was reported by Hyppolyte Taine in the preface to the third edition of his "De l'intelligence", published in 1878. Besides "etherial visions" or "magnetic auras", Fernando Pessoa claimed to have experienced automatic writing. He said he felt "owned by something else", sometimes feeling a sensation in the right arm which he claimed was lifted into the air without his will.[2]

George Hyde-Lees, the wife of William Butler Yeats, also claimed that she could write automatically.[3]

Hélène Smith claimed to have experienced automatic writing, which was included in Théodore Flouroy's *From India to the Planet Mars*. She alleged that the writing was "Martian" in origin.

William Fletcher Barrett wrote that "Automatic messages may take place either by the writer passively holding a pencil on a sheet of paper, or by the planchette, or by a 'ouija board'."[4] In spiritualism, spirits are claimed to take control of the hand of a medium to write messages, letters, and even entire books. Automatic writing can happen in a trance or waking state.[5]

Arthur Conan Doyle in his book *The New Revelation* (1918) wrote that automatic writing occurs either by the writer's subconscious or by external spirits operating through the writer.[6] The Surrealist poet Robert Desnos claimed he was among the most gifted in automatic writing. Some psychical researchers such as Thomson Jay Hudson have claimed that no spirits are involved in automatic writing and that the subconscious mind is the explanation.[7]

Alleged cases of automatic writing have included Jane Roberts,[8] Helen Schucman [9] and Neale Donald Walsch.[10][11] In 1975, Wendy Hart of Maidenhead claimed that she wrote automatically about Nicholas Moore, a sea captain who died in 1642.[12]

Scientific analysis[edit]

Scientists and skeptics consider automatic writing to be the result of the ideomotor effect.[13][14][15][16]

The physician Charles Arthur Mercier in the *British Medical Journal* (1894) criticized the spiritualist interpretation of automatic writing concluding "there is no need nor room for the agency of spirits, and the invocation of such agency is the sign of a mind not merely unscientific, but uninformed."[17] According to skeptical investigator Joe Nickell"automatic writing is produced while one is in a dissociated state. It is a form of motor automatism, or unconscious muscular activity."[18]

Psychology professor Théodore Flournoy investigated the claim by 19th-century medium Hélène Smith (Catherine Müller) that she did automatic writing to convey messages from Mars in Martian language. Flournoy concluded that her "Martian" language had a strong resemblance to Ms. Smith's native language of French and that her automatic writing was "romances of the subliminal imagination, derived largely from forgotten sources (for example, books read as a child)."

He invented the term cryptomnesia to describe this phenomenon.[19]

Automatic writing behaviour was discovered in three patients with right hemispheric damage.[20]

Connect with R. Addams

To contact R. Addams mailto:
rsqcon@yahoo.com.au

Errors in this work

We are but human after all and, despite the most stringent editing there may yet be some minor errors in this work.

Should you feel so inclined, please feel free to note any errors you find and send me the details.

I promise I won't be offended.

In fact, I admit I rushed the release of my first novel, Chaloaw Stew, to have some print copies available for a Book Show. It was the presence of minor errors in the novel, which led me to revise and re-issue the work in September 2015, and I'm grateful for the reader feedback, which highlighted a few of these errors.

R Addams